"It is impossible to classify Andrés Ne...... ....s is a new language adventure, guided by the intelligence and the pleasure of words. He never ceases to surprise us and is, doubtlessly, one of the most daring writers in Latin American literature, willing to change, challenge and explore, always with a unique elegance."—Mariana Enriquez

"*Traveler of the Century* doesn't merely respect the reader's intelligence: it sets out to worship it. . . . A beautiful, accomplished novel: as ambitious as it is generous, as moving as it is smart."
—Juan Gabriel Vásquez, *The Guardian*

"Neuman uses highly imaginative, highly poetic language to tell a cinematic story constructed like a puzzle . . . *Fracture* is a profound, captivating novel, written with confounding intelligence and wit, a heartbreakingly beautiful exploration of human consciousness."—Hélène Cardona, *World Literature Today*

"A deeply erudite but wickedly entertaining novel, with passion as well as reason in the mix, this tour-de-force from the Argentinian-born prodigy matches charming plot-twists with mind-stretching dialectic."—Boyd Tonkin, *The Independent*

"We come to see how lives are built out of passing detail, the flicker of small incidents, the intervention of literature, and the trace of forgotten things. *Talking to Ourselves* is both brilliant and wise, and Andrés Neuman is destined to be one of the essential writers of our time."—Teju Cole

"Neuman is one of the rare writers who can distill the most complex human emotions with apparent effortlessness. . . . Andrés Neuman has transcended the boundaries of geography, time, and language to become one of the most significant writers of the early twenty-first century"—*Music & Literature*

BARILOCHE

ANDRÉS NEUMAN

TRANSLATED BY ROBIN MYERS

OPEN LETTER
LITERARY TRANSLATIONS FROM THE UNIVERSITY OF ROCHESTER

Library of Congress Cataloging-in-Publication Data: Available

pb ISBN: 978-1-948830-62-1 | ebook ISBN: 978-1-948830-87-4

Support for the translation of this book was provided by Acción Cultural Española, AC/E

AC/E
ACCIÓN CULTURAL
ESPAÑOLA

Printed on acid-free paper in the United States of America.

Cover Design by Alban Fischer

Open Letter is the University of Rochester's nonprofit, literary translation press:
Lattimore Hall 411, Box 270082, Rochester, NY 14627

www.openletterbooks.org

BARILOCHE

To my parents, for the south.
To Justo Navarro, for the emotion of cold.

PROLOGUE
NEUMAN, TOUCHED BY GRACE

Among young writers who've already published a first book, Neuman may be the youngest of all, and his precocity, which comes studded with lightning bolts and proclamations, isn't his greatest virtue. Born in Argentina in 1977, but raised in Andalusia, Andrés Neuman is the author of a book of poems, *Métodos de la noche* [Night Methods], published by Hiperión in 1998, and *Bariloche*, an excellent first novel that was a finalist for the most recent Herralde Prize.

The novel is about a trash collector in Buenos Aires who works jigsaw puzzles in his spare time. I happened to be on the prize committee and Neuman's novel at once enthralled—to use an early twentieth-century term—and hypnotized me. In it, good readers will find something that can be found only in great literature, the kind written by real poets, a literature that dares to venture into the dark with open eyes and that keeps its eyes open no matter what. In principle, this is the most difficult test (also the most difficult exercise and stretch) and on no few occasions Neuman pulls it off with frightening ease. Nothing in this novel sounds contrived: everything is real, everything is an illusion. The dream in which Demetrio Rota, the Buenos Aires trash collector, moves like a sleepwalker, is the dream of great literature, and its author serves it up in precise words and scenes. When I come across these young writers it makes me want to cry. I don't know what the future holds for them. I don't know whether a drunk driver will run them down some night or whether all of a sudden they'll stop writing. If nothing like that happens, the literature of the twenty-first century will belong to Neuman and a few of his blood brothers.

Roberto Bolaño,
March 2000

It is thus that the fatigued survive.
John Berger

We live as we dream—alone.
Joseph Conrad

Sand swept away by life.
Homero Manzi

BARILOCHE: c. located on the s. shore of Lake Nahuel Huapi, Río Negro prov., 41° 19 lat. S, 71° 24' long. W. Borders Neuquén prov. Seismic station. Highest alts.: Cerro Catedral, Monte Tronador.

/

It was four o'clock sharp when Demetrio Rota weakly lit the darkness with his neon suit. Almost without thinking, he dropped a thread of spit between the sewer bars. He was pleased to hit his target. A damp gust blew in from the Río de la Plata port, crept up Independencia, and dwindled on its way to Avenida 9 de Julio, where the wintry breath of Buenos Aires swelled and thrived: dense, continuous, corrosive. The cold was the least of it.

Alongside the truck, which gave off a warm stench of engine and residue, of orange peels and old yerba mate and fuel, Demetrio Rota and his shift partner trembled with arctic indifference. Toss me those bags, toss em here, El Negro yelled. Demetrio wasn't listening. He stared down into the drain, motionless, his shoulders tensed into a shrug as if he'd forgotten to drop them. Come on man let's go, what are you doing over there. Demetrio heard him this time, but he stayed perfectly still, the bags prone at his feet like an army of grubby pets. Hey it's four oh five Demetrio, we gotta hurry or we're fucked. Then he sighed and crouched to sling the first bag to El Negro. The sewer insinuated a faraway flux.

//

Real damp, right?

Every so often El Negro would clear his nose with a sound that Demetrio found especially irritating. The sunless dawn stained the sky with the discolorations of June. Demetrio was sure the seasonal change affected El Negro, making him dumber and more talkative. As for him, it depended: some days he kept quiet, and others he liked talking about soccer and weekends or the women who walked past as the day started lifting its head.

At the end of Calle Bolívar was a cheap, shabby bar with tables shoved every which way and a few chairs scattered haphazardly around them. One was usually occupied by a slight, cheerful retiree who liked to go there for breakfast, and they knew him as the Pony. The waiter addressed him with a reverential "sir," though the Pony never drank anything but the house wine. Hey man, c'mon and take our order, we're in a hurry, El Negro declared as if the place were full. Demetrio sat pensive. It was a slow morning; they were almost fifteen minutes behind schedule and could only gulp down some cold café con leche before pressing on. The Pony sent them off with a shake of a days-old newspaper.

Thanks to a nimble El Negro, they managed to finish their route on time. Demetrio sat in the driver's seat and felt the morning's order restored to him: it helped to take off his gloves, because his fingers started feeling like fingers again and recognized the same old skin on things. He glanced in the rearview mirror at El Negro, who was collecting the last few bags with the pride of a juggler. He watched him fondly, with a slight smile, and noticed himself feeling better, almost well, as he revved up the truck. Now they'd head back to the dump to unload. Then El Negro would race off to his other job and wouldn't make it home until the afternoon, when he'd have a late lunch with his wife and measure his children's growth from the corner of his eye. Demetrio, for his part, was renting a narrow apartment near Chacarita, and after lunch he'd usually nap until the evening. He'd get up around eight, eat whatever he had lying around, and stare out the window for a while, study some cars, imagine them driving along all by themselves, without anyone in them, or else he'd choose a random rooftop to picture himself leaping off and flying away, face turned up to the cool and starless sky, until he'd get bored and sit down and get to work.

///

An open stretch of earth riddled with vast red flowers, none exactly like the rest. With dense-pressed grass and stalwart midday light, the field takes on the quality of a soft flag. Beside it, at a distance from the cabin, the lake unfolds. Its steady gleam goes dull as it advances toward the ridge. There isn't much to see of all the mountains yet: just a rough outline of the peaks, tall index fingers pointing into space, identifying the unnavigable routes. The cabin was the classic alpine model with two small, slightly uneven windows. Meanwhile, two cats playacted scratches and affection, jumbling their colors. Ancient, the tree bark seems to bear sole witness to the passing years, amid so much eternal water and so many flowers dying young.

IV

The truck didn't sound good when it started up. Demetrio noticed right away and told El Negro, who looked unfazed and told him to drive. Whatever you say Negro but this thing's going to leave us high and dry. The engine coughed a little and the truck lurched into motion.

Demetrio's drowsiness smeared the pavement. The stoplights stained the symmetries of traffic. El Negro looked at him from the passenger seat and said nothing. He knew that Demetrio would sharpen and brighten as the morning wore on, his eyes beginning to gleam with anxious lucidity. His replies would grow less laconic, and as it came time to retrace toward the dump, El Negro would almost regret having to part ways. He was used to Demetrio's transformations: first a sleepwalker, then his trademark indifference, then a reaction calibrated to the morning itself, and then that desperate loquaciousness, an urgency in how he got in and out of the truck or shouted through the window.

They'd had a good breakfast, but Demetrio's stomach felt hollow as a well. He pictured his lunch as he walked. His sense of touch and smell prickled in him, asserting themselves with every movement. His tongue felt soft in his mouth. Blistered potatoes, tomatoes bursting scarlet, an obscene, succulent steak before plunging into bed, rubbing his face, his thighs against the sheets, smiling, exhausted; then unconsciousness. Demetrio opened the door to the building. At the end of the hall, he saw that the elevator was still out of order. He endured the steep stairs all the way up to the sixth floor. When he stepped into the apartment, a hazy calm fondled his mind.

IV

He opened his eyes at a quarter to eight and found darkness. His muscles ached when he sat up. He exhaled several times, put on his sneakers, and shuffled into the kitchen, where he heated coffee and poured himself a generous cup. Without tasting it, he went to the window to watch the cars go by. The shop lights glimmered like buoys demarcating a shipwreck. People walked with a homeward stride.

He sipped the coffee slowly, feeling it travel through him. He tried to imagine some benevolent effect. It provided a measure of satisfaction. He left the cup in the sink, sat down at the table in the living room, and took the rectangular box into his hands.

Behind the cabin, several pine trees fluttered slender arms in greeting. The upright patience of the trunks, the planks in parallel, the rippling of the lakes and paths, dialogued in rapt geometry. The brilliant beams distributed the shadows in equal portions.

Demetrio studied the hole in the upper left corner: it looked like God had taken a bite there. He reached into the box and spilled some pieces onto the table. He closed his eyes and pressed his thumb, middle, and index fingers into them, then released the pressure. The cabin lingered in his sight, the pathways muddled with the lake, lit shards behind his lids. He looked down at the landscape again. He chose a piece at random, gauged its color, and ventured where it should go: it fit. Good, good. Not much longer now. He tried another: no luck.

He got up and went back to the window. He couldn't see anyone on the street. Living in Chacarita was strange. There, you could feel the full weight of the night, its peculiar silence after a whole day of coming and going and buses and murmurs and open stores and candied-nut vendors on the corners, so different from how things had been before. Once, a long time ago, he'd lived in Lanús, where his neighbors were in cahoots or at least enemies, where every dog could be identified and the streets were a pretext for kids to be all over and everywhere. In Lanús, almost no one had any money to paint their houses or go to the beach in the summer or buy the clothes you needed to take over the world. And before the before, he'd been even farther away, much farther away from the capital and its turbulence: in a place where things grew joyfully and aged with calm. Demetrio had experienced the former. Learning to swim in the Nahuel

Huapi, learning not to freeze to death in the Nahuel Huapi, learning about the silence of the Nahuel Huapi, studying in a little brick schoolhouse near Llao Llao, playing soccer wherever. There the myrtles were like no others and the chocolate tasted vaguely of Europe in the snow.

He turned away from the street and regarded the cabin landscape from where he stood. He shook his head. Stretching his limbs, he felt a comforting tickle and an abrupt acuity, as if it were suddenly a different time of day. He returned to the table: the most important part was still missing from the sky.

VI

As they rested, sitting on the curb, Demetrio dissected one of the bags. It was partway open and smelled both bitter and rotten. Unrepulsed, he peeled back the edge of the bag and peered inside. He could see several green bottles and bits of meat, minced or perhaps gnawed by a dog; the mixture was slathered in some sort of dairy product. Demetrio released the bag, disappointed. This was another habit that El Negro couldn't make sense of but silently respected. There were mornings when Demetrio treated the residue with a distance akin to condemnation, while other mornings he showed up looking different, disconcertingly calm, and set out to investigate, meticulous as a watchmaker.

All of a sudden, he stopped. Then he dug around a little more and focused on something inside the bag. El Negro didn't speak, but he knew Demetrio would, any moment now, and so he waited. Extracting a series of objects, Demetrio looked at him obliquely and held out his right hand. El Negro leaned in and saw Demetrio's gloves clasping a small head with red hair, an armless torso, and a tiny left leg that still evoked an ancient tenderness. The rest wasn't there, at least not in this bag, and it didn't seem wise to expect additional parts to appear in the others. Demetrio murmured: you see, Negro, you see? El Negro stared at the discolored head, the autonomous leg, the diminutive torso, and then looked Demetrio right in the eye, trusting this would suffice as an expression of agreement. Then Demetrio procured several curls of orange peel, wrapped them around the pieces of the doll, and returned them carefully to the bag.

The confusing mix of hunger and fatigue produced a strange soft taste in Demetrio's mouth when he swallowed. He ambled home as if he were going somewhere else. He'd gotten off a couple stops before his, almost without realizing what he'd done. When he came to the Lacroze station and saw the Chacarita cemetery on his left, rigid and tenacious, he decided he hadn't yet walked far enough, this landscape had come too soon, he should have gotten off much earlier or even taken the entire route on foot. He watched people streaming from the mouth of the subway, vomited out onto the street, stepping forth into the open air. For an instant, Demetrio felt an urge to go down the stairs and make his way in, to travel the streets of the neighborhood from below. But he continued on, skirted the cemetery, and turned right a little before the Tronador station. His legs and eyelids felt equally heavy.

He woke twice in the evening. Once his bladder forced him to; the second time he'd simply opened his eyes. He didn't dawdle at the window for long. He sat down at the living room table and felt the tiny shapes in his hand. The missing reflections in the lake were easy to conjure and Demetrio wasn't worried about them. He was troubled only by that hole in the sky. He dropped a fistful of loose pieces and probed them one by one with his index finger, seeking their most favorable profile. The flowers weren't finished, but Demetrio studied and sniffed them, thumbed their petals. He wanted to catch the cats, but they were impossibly swift and he gave up. The air perfumed his breath and made it nearly tangible. He closed his eyes and heard a voice calling his name: he wasn't sure if he should respond or flee. Suddenly he broke into a run and rolled around in the earth that led into town, smearing his knees and palms, sensing the tranquil closeness of the lake and a distant voice wearily repeating the name he so despised.

VII

Intermittently rainy, discontinuous, the trash pickup felt strange the next morning. The sequence of minutes, the cleansed asphalt of Avenida Independencia, the docility of the residual plastic that seemed, rather than resisting with its weight, to help them lift the bags and heap them together—it all suggested another order, a different breath. As for the truck, it was literally different: the usual one was being disemboweled by the company mechanics and would be out of commission for a few days. The tires plowed the wet filth of the narrow Calle Defensa, channel of clumsy and laborious passage. Working the last shift had one advantage, Demetrio thought: you got to witness the morning's gestation, the origin of everything that would form the lattice of what people called a business day, these hours that Demetrio could barely glimpse as he rode the bus downtown from the mother mountain of waste, or as he waited for the 93 that would take him all the way back to Chacarita to bolt down his premature lunch and furiously surrender to sleep.

Around six, they'd found a kid digging around in the garbage, bearing the gray rain on his shoulders. El Negro had asked if he had a dad or older brother who could give him a hand, what was he up to so early all by himself? Nobody tells me what to do and what do you care if I'm alone, besides you're doing the same thing as me and you're real old, I'm gonna rob a bank when I grow up and get way far away from here, I'm going to the beach where the sun stays out all year long. Listen kid why don't you come with me and we'll take you for some grub and coffee, Jesus Christ.

They'd sat him down at a table in the bar on Calle Bolívar. The Pony had stared at them, baffled, and lifted his first empty glass of the morning. Hey waiter get this kid some café con leche and a medialuna, okay?, a medialuna or a sandwich if he wants. Is he your son? No you idiot how the fuck would he be my son, you think I'd drag him out of bed to haul shit around with me?, shut up man you're killing me, and don't you forget I may not dress my kids in fancy clothes or whatever but they're clean, you hear? You want a ham and cheese sandwich? The boy nodded with the reticence of someone familiar with the improbability of simple favors in San Telmo at a quarter to seven in the morning. And somehow, Demetrio sensed, the kid's suspicions were well-founded: more than feeding him, El Negro was sating some dark unease in the monstrous faces of his two sons, or in his own.

They hadn't spoken a word between them on their way back to the dump. El Negro drove and Demetrio counted the raindrops on the windshield. The new truck sounded good and drove easy and was probably far superior to the ancient, discontinued Mercedes that had been their companion for so long, but it felt too unfamiliar for them to get attached. Demetrio glanced at El Negro, who looked pale. Listen Negro of course you kicked him out, what the fuck else were you going to do, I mean it's not like you could let him nick your wallet once you'd already paid for his breakfast, don't beat yourself up about it, come on. El Negro was even paler.

They switched off the silent engine of the new truck and got out. A few flimsy drops still pattered down, failing to dampen their neon suits. The manager told them just a second. When another truck like theirs turned and headed for the garage, the man motioned and they started the engine again and drove up to the fenced abyss to unload the hundreds of pounds of waste that could barely take the edge off the greed of that reeking maw. Before he said goodbye to El Negro, Demetrio opened the glove compartment and took out two misshapen scraps of rough leather, each with a vertical zipper. What the fuck is that Demetrio? He held out the boots to offer a better look. El Negro shrugged.

VIII

Breaking with habit, he showered before dinner. He let the water redeem his pores, eyes closed, listening to the stream's monotonous prayer. He examined his body as he soaped himself: he had more hair than a few years ago, yet his skin looked more helpless than before, less willing; his thighs had retained some of their trapezoidal shape and an acceptable volume that encouraged him to keep inspecting; he observed the thicket of pubic hair with his member slipping out, folded into itself like a strange larva. More out of pride than anything else, he shook it a bit and waited for it to straighten up, lazy. Then he turned off the faucet and dried himself.

Instead of eating right away, he stood engrossed at the window, trying to recover the volatile sense of well-being he'd had before he fell asleep, a vague satisfaction that predisposed him to benevolence and made the most basic needs feel desirable—eating, sleeping, shitting—while also dismissing his earlier foul mood as foolish. Before long, a shiver of reality crept through him. Then he went to the kitchen and began, methodically and indifferently, to chew. He went to his room in search of some shabby black boots and daubed them with polish. He imagined he was stroking the flank of an exhausted colt, and he could almost hear the skin respond, refreshed, to the damp ointment. He studied the gleaming makeup on the worn hide and figured chance had winked at him. He carefully pulled on the boots, noting their stiff disfigurement.

He went to the living room table and sat down facing the cabin and the lake and the paths. He reached out a hand and picked up a solitary shard of clouds, a sprig of trimmed white gases: he would have to fuse it into the sweeping sky. He calculated where the distant reflection of the Nahuel Huapi had to come from, the shadows on the cabin door. It was true, he confirmed: a certain steady, distant voice called out to him at regular intervals, as he hid behind a trunk that wasn't a myrtle and smelled of time. How many days had he waded along the shore in his black boots, how many menacing forecasts of pneumonia were never fulfilled, much to the indignation of that ever-furrowed brow. Cutting wood had always been his best excuse for freedom, the axe resting on his shoulder as if allowing itself to be comforted, the blade giving him a fatalistic tickle on the neck. It was the same axe that had so often given him an excuse to hide from the redheaded girl, bloody and smiling invincibly, with a vocation for flight, but also with the voracious curiosity of fire-beings, the wonderment he'd seize as an opportunity to flaunt his axe with military flair, trying to control his spasms of desire and fear. Amid the birds' orchestral commotion, the monotonous voice that kept calling his name would usually vanish into some ridiculous detail.

IX

She was older than me. She dressed like the local guys, hiding her body as much as she could. She didn't live too far, but I saw that stretch of dirt and sometimes mud as a whole ceremony, a distance I couldn't cross just like that. I was always terrified when I set out, and halfway there I'd take a detour to play it cool, and then I'd wander over to the Nahuel and toss rocks into the water, thinking there was no point in suffering like this, maybe I should just go back to the cabin, and then somehow I'd find myself on the dirt path again and my heart would pound under my jacket. I'd ignore my fear and keep walking as I pictured scenes of lust that mixed together with the most callow kind of love. And suddenly I'd see her all by herself, sitting on a stump, bam!, there she was, my redhead. I'd wave hello or waggle my axe like an idiot, as if I'd had to come all this way to cut wood instead of just going out into the field by my house. I don't know if she noticed or if she was really always as distracted as she seemed, but she'd wave back and wait for me to trudge my way over. If it wasn't too cold, we'd walk in the woods, and before we started up the slope I always wondered if I'd ever dare to grab her around the waist, bold as I'd never been, and kiss her at last, not trembling anymore.

X

In the garage that morning, Demetrio had to wait a long
time for El Negro to show up. Surveying the trucks in
search of his own, he saw one with a flat tire. He peered
all around the enormous depot, which looked like a funeral
home for elephants, and saw that the manager was engrossed
with his transistor radio. So Demetrio crouched down and
calmly deflated the three other wheels of the truck. Then
he removed two valves and slipped them into his pocket.
He glanced back at the manager and approached the next
vehicle. This time he deflated one tire almost completely
and let just a little air out of another. Right away, he realized
it had been stupid of him to ruin all four tires of a single
truck—but it would prove even more stupid, he told himself, if they suspected one of the drivers, who were all well
versed in the travails of mobilizing these mastodons. Only
then, having already acted on impulse, did Demetrio sense
the possible motive for his behavior: to make the mechanics
rush to fix his old truck, so they could move on to the other

vehicles. He was thoroughly convinced by this revelation, he felt just and redemptive. He deflated three more tires on different trucks.

El Negro arrived almost twenty minutes late, which was so unusual that Demetrio hugged him when El Negro appeared, harrumphing his way over from the far end of the garage, belly jiggling. What's up Negro? My wife's a slut, that's what's up. Don't say that you moron, she's crazy about you and you know it! I'm telling you that's what she is Demetrio you don't get it man, hurry up or we're fucked, come on. Okay fine but look slow down and tell me what's going on because this is crazy talk Negro. What do you know. Demetrio felt a flash of guilt about the tires when the engine started. As they drove toward the exit, the manager waved an absent hand through the window of his booth, his ear still pressed to the radio.

Listen Negro are you sure though? Look sometimes you get the wrong idea and then you have to apologize. El Negro shook his head theatrically. The Pony ordered another red wine and chuckled to himself. Talk to me Negro, come on. What do you want me to say, I'm telling you she went and fucked some guy and now she has the nerve to come crying to me, and since I'm a fucking idiot I comfort her instead of beating the shit outta her, just wait till I get home. Demetrio flashed on El Negro's wife: a few years younger than him, very dark hair, always trying some new diet, too much makeup. She certainly wasn't beautiful, but she gave off something between helpless and provocative that stirred a certain anxiety or agitation in men. She was a sharp woman, an affectionate woman, and worst of all: she was more educated than her husband. Don't freak out Negro, I mean think about it she must get lonely when you're not around, all those hours apart every day, you probably can't even imagine how bad she misses you, poor thing. El Negro kept shaking his round whiskered head, but Demetrio thought he glimpsed a doubt thawing in his eyes, his jaw loosening.

XI

Already overcome with hunger, Demetrio remembered his fridge at home was empty. He'd studied the daily lunch menu on the small Coca-Cola chalkboard and felt his pants pocket, knowing he barely had enough but wouldn't hesitate to go in anyway. He'd stressed to the waiter that the meat should be slightly overdone and the salad couldn't have onion and, if possible, the coffee should be half cold milk. Sluggish, he now crossed the Plaza de Mayo toward Alem and wondered whether he should stray from his usual itinerary. Suddenly he saw the 93 bus hurtling toward him; by the time he returned to himself, he was gripping the back of a sticky plastic seat, drowning in the deluge of passengers, watching the Avenida del Libertador stretch out longer and longer. He yearned to be back in Chacarita and at home and in bed, on the brink of sleep, and he thought maybe he was, for a few moments he almost pulled it off, but then he was forced to accept that the traffic was awful, that it was hot even though it was winter, and that he was being trod, shoved, and trampled again.

He felt his way around the apartment as if probing the walls of a sanctuary. The kitchen tiles trembled with fatigue. He went to the bathroom, pissed with relish, took off his shoes, stroked his pillow, breathed between the sheets, the sheets were dissolving into something else, becoming water, becoming waves.

When the tachycardia of his alarm informed him what was happening, Demetrio jolted upright with a vague nostalgia for the middle of the day. He groped at the foot of his bed and felt the old leather of the black boots. He put them on and went to the kitchen, boiled a couple of eggs, glanced at the clock: nine-thirty. He swallowed the eggs, which tasted of gummy nothingness, and went to the window once again. In his smoking days, he recalled, the streets usually allowed themselves to be contemplated; each gray exhalation seemed to match the pulse of the vehicles, the corners. Now that cigarettes meant a stranger's occasional kindness or an alien luxury, the scrap of neighborhood framed by his window didn't look the same; it was more exhausted, less harmonious as it puttered along between predictable lines that never fully resembled those fickle bluish drawings. He sighed unthinkingly as if breathing out the smoke of before. He turned his back on the traffic and the absent neon of shuttered storefronts.

He sat down at the table to study the handful of pieces, the punctured sky of the landscape. The gaps were growing intelligible, the flowers were complete, and the grass, gleaming and unkempt, only half hid the cats' dispute. The day was still bright, but if you focused on the flanks of the lake, you could glimpse the coming dusk. Demetrio knew that moment well, and he looked down at his boots as if they were a wrinkled prophecy. The sky was closing up.

XII

That sad night blinded me.

The last hours of Friday were always the freest. Our parents would loosen up a little and let us come back late if we'd done our homework during the week. I wasn't a goody-goody, one of those kids who was all yes mommy and couldn't find their own balls, but I got by and didn't give the teachers much to complain about. After I'd had a snack, I liked to go down to the Nahuel even if it was cold out. The lake was like a huge water-brother who understood me without asking for anything in return. That time I'd gone to skip stones on the bank. My feet were damp in my boots and I wasn't sure what time it was. Then I see this thick jacket approaching and an unmistakable shock of hair, red as sunset on the Nahuel, and I play dumb and keep tossing rocks, waiting to see if she calls out to me before I say anything. At first I didn't think she would, but then suddenly she goes and yells, Hey Demetrio, want to come smoke by the stumps? I meant to say no at first, play hard to get, but instead I just waved my arms like an imbecile and ran along the shore until I caught up with her.

It was incredible to be looking right at her without getting nervous. At least smoking weed gave us something to do, so we could pretend to be silent on purpose and smoke better, focus better. Her hair was messy and the reddish whirls fell lightly onto her shoulders. She started to cough, and I wasn't exactly an expert smoker either, so I go and sort of pat her on the back and sort of hug her a little, I don't know, and she kind of wriggles away but also leans closer, and there's a moment when she's still coughing but isn't choking or anything, and then we stare at each other and we're very serious, not saying anything, and that was the first time I ever saw her look as scared as me, and prettier than ever, and I don't know how, I think mostly just to stop feeling so awkward, I just kiss her and breathe into her mouth, and she grips me and presses hard into me and then we didn't look at each other anymore because everything happened in the dark, me on top of her with my jacket still on, slipping a hand under her clothes and finding her cold tits. I didn't really know what I was doing but I just went for it, pulling down her jeans the best I could, and she let me without either helping or resisting, just panted hard and kissed me with a kind of desperation. And once I was all set, when I could feel the skin of her legs brushing against my hips, it happened: panic filled my chest and paralyzed my blood, it clouded my vision and flooded my thoughts with other things that had nothing to do with any of it, and regret came, too, I wanted to scream or be back at home eating my afternoon snack or just be another idiot like all those idiots who spend all day doing their homework, and I stopped listening to her breath and feeling her legs and started hearing the sound of every little bug and creature that lived in the forest. I kept moving a little while longer, alone, with a body below me, as all the cold of the night and all the fear and then all the shame melted together into one still point inside me.

XIII

Always more vivid in his memory than when Demetrio found himself actually there, Avenida Independencia was still deserted. The occasional insomniac taxi or bus drove by. As Demetrio and El Negro hoisted bags on the corner of Calle Perú and Calle Chile, a swift, murky-colored shape materialized amid a pile of polyethylene and food scraps, making them leap back and shield their faces. They could make out the entrails of a bag through a savage gash in the plastic. An instant later, another terse silhouette sprang out and joined the first before they scattered, playfully, like two delirious marionettes. Demetrio shivered. They resumed their collection in silence, as if they'd had the same dream of two cats.

El Negro had been acting just like his old self since the day he'd showed up late to work, which was exactly what made Demetrio suspect that something was wrong: his partner was trying too hard to work efficiently, to whistle at women when the light changed, to burst into uproarious laughter. Demetrio was afraid to ask, but he imagined nights of shouting, of putting the kids to bed early because there's school tomorrow sweet dreams kiddos, before turning off the light and carrying on with the rage and the mutual accusations in which El Negro would always have the last word.

They went into the bar on Bolívar and immediately noticed that the Pony wasn't there. The waiter seemed restless, as if the desolation of the place had revealed itself to him in the absence of the Pony's three or four early glasses of wine. Morning kid, two sandwiches and two coffees, mine black cause I'm beat, El Negro declared, settling in at the bar. Meanwhile, Demetrio went to the bathroom and situated himself at the urinal with his feet set wide apart. At the sight of the faint warm steam, he was pierced by a distant sense of guilt.

In the garage, they received the news that their old truck had been repaired and tuned up. They patted each other on the back, satisfied, and parted ways. El Negro rushed off to his other job; Demetrio made his way downtown. He got off the bus at Marcelo T. de Alvear and walked along Libertad, a far cleaner and less familiar street than the ones he usually wandered. He came to a shopping center and stopped in front of an enormous toy store. When he didn't see what he was looking for in the window display, he went in and asked the clerk, who brought him three different boxes. Demetrio immediately ruled out the first, a ridiculous snowy forest. Dubious, almost worried, he regarded the second box. Then he focused hard on the third. He looked at it for a long time without making the slightest gesture or saying a single word. The gray sack of the sky was about to rupture over the pines. The light churned restlessly on the lake. The clerk seemed uncomfortable and began attending to other customers as they came in. Demetrio held the box in both hands like a stone figurine.

He went straight to the living room table as soon as he closed the apartment door behind him. He observed the ancient landscape, perfect at long last; the sky was dense, each bloom was in its place, the cabin offered sturdy strength and smoke against the cold, the lake spread outward undisturbed. To the window came the undulating supplication of a meow. He set the box he'd bought on the table, carefully put away the finished landscape, and got into bed without lunch, stealing a glance at the black boots, crushed together at the foot of the bed.

XIV

The stiff leaves, sweet-scented papyruses. A single side of the green triangle: perhaps the canopy. The shore with its descending stones. Vegetal cracks. A gray-white fury, split, above the peaks. Sporadic creases in the water's sheen. The storm is on its way.

The araucarias raise hands that slowly find their shape. Beyond them, yellow, sundered into scraps, still scattered: an amancay, perhaps. Some purple swaths of lake are ruffled, come and go before the storm coheres. There's no horizon, only surface. And everything's a hue in transformation.

There also seems to be a narrow shadow, leafage of some kind. But he hadn't remembered any cedar there.

XV

At the age when a boy is supposed to start looking like a man, Mario Miguel Fernando, alias the Pony, had opened a newsstand and stopped reading the papers.

Both his older brother and his father had been newspapermen and his grandfather had sold newspapers, too; as for the Pony's great-grandfather, no one remembered him. Sheltered by the zinc sheets of his stall on Calle Alsina, he sometimes thought about how he would have liked to teach the business to his son, if he'd had one. It was a simple but serious trade: you had to wake unfailingly before dawn, five minutes before your alarm, so you'd already be dressed when it went off and thus resist the temptation to keep sleeping. You had to eat breakfast whenever and however you could. Running a newsstand meant learning to caress the paper without blackening your fingertips with ink (like touching a woman, kid, like touching a woman, he'd have told his son once he was old enough to have a nickname of his own or else inherit his father's forever). Most of all, it meant learning how to gauge exactly when to volunteer a suggestion to an indecisive page-turner or to stay silent so as not to make him uncomfortable; to distinguish reliable customers from people who should never be sold a newspaper on credit. Bearded customers especially: his father had taught him that a man who doesn't shave will never be a man's man.

Readers of the news, the Pony maintained, hold the intimate conviction that the news is actually about them. He himself had stopped reading the papers when he realized they'd never have anything to do with his own affairs: that's when he became a bona fide newspaperman. From then on, the years could be very short if you counted the days of the week according to the front pages of *La Nación*, *Clarín*, or *Crónica*: Monday the 23rd, Tuesday the 24th, Wednesday the 25th, and the stacks of paper fell and rose and fell again. Like people do.

Every day, the Pony brought his yerba mate and a red thermos to the newsstand. Between customers, he'd pour himself a couple bitter infusions with a steady hand and suck them dry in one deep draw, hollowing out his clean-shaven cheeks. Then he'd exhale the lingering heat of the liquid into the cold air and sit watching the steam wisp itself into nothing. This, under his blue zinc roof, smoking the morning away, was how the Pony had spent thirty years awaiting the right time for a good glass of red or a good death.

XVI

They hadn't seen the Pony for four mornings in a row. The waiter didn't mention him, and Demetrio and El Negro didn't either, which made his absence from the corner even more conspicuous. That morning, however, they weren't alone: a middle-aged woman with an air of resignation had come in for breakfast. She murmured that she'd just dropped off her daughter at school and lowered her harried buttocks onto one of the revolving chairs. Her outfit seemed slightly out of context: it wasn't a standard look for shopping or similar tasks, although it wasn't really elegant, either. Her own vaguely awkward expression seemed to confirm this. Demetrio flinched when he realized her resemblance to El Negro's wife and turned cautiously toward him—just in time to glimpse a wild look in El Negro's eyes that immediately contracted into his standard wink. Demetrio insisted on picking up the check. They emerged into the stubborn cold of Calle Bolívar.

You coming to La Bombonera on Sunday? We're playing El Ciclón and we're gonna school em, we're gonna tear em a new one, you'll see. I can't, Negro, sorry, I'm busy on Sunday, don't get all pissed, I'll come to the next one, promise. Give me a fuckin break, you sellout, you call yourself a Boca fan. I really can't, Negro. And you call yourself a Boca fan. They parked the truck among the others, took off their uniforms, and said goodbye. Demetrio watched El Negro sprinting downhill (shit, I'm not gonna make it, look what time it is, that bus always takes forever) with an ungainliness he found endearing, crucial. Once his partner was out of sight, Demetrio set out unhurriedly on foot, past the overflowing pit they fed a little more each day. He stared out at the crazed mosaic, transfixed by its exhausted colors. For a moment it felt like he and the abyss were yawning in unison.

The Friday frenzy was a tangible thing. Pedestrians and bus passengers scuffled almost enthusiastically over the same opaque, manhandled air of all the other days. Squinting, observing the hard brakes and zealous lurches, Demetrio savored the weekend in advance and imagined a kind of contentment only possible on Friday afternoon, when leisure is still an unbroken promise.

XVII

The blinds, a giant's heavy lids, revealed a clotted sky. Its shoddy light degraded every object into whitishness. Annoyed, Demetrio remembered the Saturday that sleep had just annihilated. He hadn't gone out for a walk, he hadn't given the newspaper a leisurely read, the hours had stampeded away from him. He hadn't even sat down to work at the table. He had, however, eaten off-schedule, watched TV almost without paying attention, gone to bed at night like everyone else, and, in sum, had hated his day off. He left his room with the dim suspicion that he'd been scammed. He ate an apathetic breakfast. Little by little, he registered the obese impact of consciousness: it was Sunday, tense morning, afternoon of soccer and shouting, of Bombanera stadium, of betrayal.

He showered and dressed more carefully than usual, elected not to eat lunch, left the black boots by the door for his return that night, and went out. Chacarita was blanching. The sleepy traffic foundered. As he reached the bus stop,

Demetrio saw an old man hunched over a cane who looked like the Pony and seemed to be watching him. He lifted his face toward the sky and received a viscous note of light, the cold ruffling his wet hair. He lowered his eyes and scanned the streets: the city shrugged. So he decided to stop waiting and descended into the mouth of the Lacroze subway station. The panorama grew murkier the deeper he went. He felt like the old man was following him and quickened his pace. He walked, turned around a couple times, let himself be transported by an underground staircase, and reached the platform. He peered into the silence of the cave. There was nothing at first. Then a slowly expanding dot and a growing tremor began to announce themselves, and the screech grew shriller and he found himself dazzled by a powerful eye as the steel melted into a clamor that rose and multiplied until it flooded the platform, deafening him. The doors opened and Demetrio let himself step in. For a moment, when the machine revved into motion and he sat still, he couldn't remember where he was going.

He got off at Carlos Pellegrini and emerged into the washed-out midday light. He thought of continuing on foot, but his laziness dissuaded him. He caught the bus to Parque Lezama and took his time crossing it: the city made more sense to him there, an oasis of sorts, a blissful Sunday bright with voices and bicycles and the scent of caramel apple, a dancing axis dotted with horses that flew and sank, ridden by tiny revolving riders, and groups of kids chasing the dream of a plastic ball, tireless swings, shouts exchanging hands, and ice cream vendors, and numberless trees. Demetrio lingered at the edges of the park, treading hard on the leaves and the earth. As soon as he crossed the road, he sped up again and reached La Boca, coming to a street he knew well, old train tracks coated in grass, some precarious asphalt, and a corner where he would wait, hidden, until El Negro emerged from the building, bound for Bombanera stadium.

Demetrio left at six on the dot, even though he knew El Negro wouldn't be back until seven or even later, if his friends were drunk or the team had won. He retraced, walking back over the same rusty and impassable tracks. He could still smell the scent of sweat and quasi-French perfume. His inner thighs pulsed. He sensed a pleasant heat under his belly and an echoing brush against the sides of his buttocks. He felt the sting of teeth on his neck, a snarl of hair in his hands, a thick, bittersweet tang at the back of his tongue. But rising above all these tiny comforts sounded a final voice, dull and deep, imposing itself, dictating disgust: disgust for himself and the premature night, for yet another Sunday, for feeling such base indifference at the thought of the next morning and El Negro.

XVIII

The amancay exudes a misty, wheat-hued silhouette. The ancient sky is clearer where the araucaria reaches to. The bark is chiaroscuro-dappled. The clouds' strange rustling sifts into the left-hand side, the shore-side, and menaces the sky-blue swaths. And something new: the mastheads of a pine grove start to surface on the other shore. The future trace of the horizon will suspend the spread of water; up above, the brawny dorsals of the mountain range, that great osseous reptile. But for now, only a milky cold, a summit taking shape.

Sometimes he wonders if there couldn't be, in some secluded corner of the landscape, behind the amancay, perhaps, perched on a boulder by the shore, a haunting figure, pale-faced in the shadows, reddish tresses rippling till the wind sweeps her away: those copper threads he had desired, touched, and smelled one frozen dusk.

The storm throngs closer, widening its gaseous black insides. The water travels, roughs its course.

XIX

He fixed his eyes on El Negro as they finished putting on their uniforms. A strong wind assailed them in gusts. The waste seemed to have fermented overnight, and the stench staggered even the most experienced among their guild. Demetrio watched his partner struggle with the zipper, then helped him and said they'd better hurry up. El Negro nodded brusquely. They got into the truck and set out.

Know what, she learned her lesson my wife, she even looks different, listen to this, I know her like the back of my hand and that's the truth, I gave her all the shit I wanted and she just sat and took it, I hollered my head off for a whole week and she was all quiet, just sitting there listening. I know I said at first I was gonna go and beat the shit out of her, but what can I say Demetrio, you forgive if you want to get forgiven, plus she's right, how can I go fuck up my kids' lives when they're still growing up, and then there's the house after all these years, I mean would I move out or what? would I go live in some whole other house?, no fuckin way. She went and fucked the first guy she could find cause she was sad and lonely, right?, and in my own house, that's what fuckin kills me the most!, but I'm not stupid, I figured it out right away when I saw her changing the sheets even though she'd just changed them yesterday, so you're gonna dupe me, huh?, so you think I'm an idiot or what do you think exactly. And then that was the end of it, right?, I gave her hell and if you'd seen her Demetrio I swear you wouldn't even recognize her, all ashamed crying on her knees that she loved me and we weren't gonna ruin all those faithful years for one little mistake, were we? Now she's cooking all this great food like at the beginning and she's always waiting for me in bed. Demetrio nodded and said good job Negro, placing a hand on his shoulder.

Calle Defensa vanished into its hall-like narrowness. On the corner of Calle México, a strange and sudden noise made Demetrio fumble intently at the bag. He pulled off his gloves, undid the knot, and found some shards of porcelain at the bottom. It was a small dessert plate that had fractured into three pieces. A dish from an old tea-serving household. Demetrio knelt, placed the pieces on the ground, and arranged them closer together: he discovered that it was missing a triangle. He rummaged impatiently in the bag and found nothing. So he fit the shards together as best he could, tied the bag again, and got into the truck, leaving the porcelain dish behind, served to the solitary cold of Calle Defensa.

XX

The Pony's wake was at ten o'clock on Wednesday morning and his burial at eight the next day. Demetrio and El Negro, informed by the downcast waiter, informed in turn by who knows who, had agreed to talk on the phone and see about going to the wake together. El Negro needed to make sure he could take the day off at his other job. In the end they couldn't grant him permission, or at least that's what they said, since they were unable to verify that the deceased was a close relative. Then Demetrio and El Negro tried their luck with the waste collection company, which replied that they could certainly attend the funeral so long as they didn't mind having an hour and a half (two, rounding up) deducted from their pay: six thirty to eight, the official unloading period at the dump. Demetrio suggested bumping up their shift a bit, starting earlier that morning. El Negro replied that he came home too exhausted to sleep any less than he already did, and the company seconded his response, arguing that the same truck—the one the two of them had already insisted so emphatically on driving—would still be in use, only becoming available during their usual hours. And, in any case, any modification to the shift schedule and vehicle distribution would entail a total reconfiguration of the organizational chart, a task the company was unable to perform. In the end, it was decided that Demetrio and El Negro would cut their shift short and have a couple hours lopped off their wages. Neither seemed satisfied.

They'd undertaken the collection at a vengeful plod, dawdling as long as they could on Calle Defensa, ponderously counting the bags on the corner of Venezuela and Perú. After unloading, they left the truck badly parked. They'd changed their clothes and drenched themselves in cologne. Then they'd taken a bus downtown and split a taxi that seemed to participate in every bottleneck in the city before leaving them, mildly late, at the entrance to the Chacarita cemetery. The burial hadn't started yet. Attendance was sparse: eight or nine people, counting the priest, the two gravediggers, Demetrio, El Negro, and the waiter, who'd kept the bar closed that day in the spirit of mourning. Someone else was also waiting for the ceremony to begin, a strange little man in a moth-eaten suit, carrying a briefcase.

Demetrio saw the gravediggers signal to the priest, who started out at a slow walk, head bowed. Everyone else, including the little man, followed the coffin, which advanced on the shoulders of two cemetery workers. During the procession toward the burial plot, they heard the first and only sobs, half-muffled by an ancient black-clad woman who stooped even lower to conceal her grief. She quieted quickly when no one joined her. That's when the waiter approached them. Demetrio was jarred to see him in a suit and tie instead of his usual bow tie; his shirt and pants looked like the same ones he always wore at the bar. I didn't think, he remarked in a confidential tone, that the Pony had a wife. Well yeah, El Negro replied, poor guy was always alone, of course we didn't think he was married. No, no, I mean the Pony told me. Told you what? That he was a widower!

During the priest's mechanical prayers, Demetrio felt or assumed he should dedicate a final memory to the Pony. He wanted to evoke him fondly among the empty tables of the bar on Bolívar, but he found himself struggling to picture his face. He knew he'd had a fine head of gray hair, which was almost always invisible beneath his newsie cap; he remembered the watery gleam of his close-set eyes, his shrill, slightly tremulous voice—but what did his face look like as a whole? He leaned in and whispered his question to El Negro, who shushed him with a finger to his lips. The gravediggers motioned for the widow to toss a bit of earth onto the coffin where her husband lay. Her husband, meanwhile (this thought suddenly struck Demetrio), was surely missing his final morning wine. As soon as the prayers were over, the priest and the workers vanished and the group dispersed in silence.

Just before they left the cemetery, they were approached by the little man, who'd been sniffing around during the entire service. He set down his briefcase and introduced himself: my name is so-and-so. Perplexed, Demetrio and El Negro glanced at each other and asked what he wanted. The little man held out his hand. Nothing, he said; his sole mission was to determine whether or not the time off they'd requested was in fact due to the death of a family member or close friend, a matter that had been satisfactorily verified and, thus, his duty fulfilled. And it was only out of respect for the widow that he hadn't left earlier and also, in part, because he quite liked funerals, actually. With that, he gave them both another firm handshake, picked up his briefcase, and disappeared, as they both trudged slowly toward the gate.

XXI

For once, Demetrio didn't have a long walk home. El Negro had left immediately for his other job with his distinctive gait: both stumbling and swift, both clumsy and resolute. Demetrio stuffed his hands into his pockets and felt as if he were returning from a long journey that required him to recognize things again: the vicinity of Federico Lacroze, the jam-packed 93 buses, the neglected sidewalks, the eroded edges of street corners, the indeterminate drizzle that muddled Chacarita even when the weather seemed good.

As he walked, he found that he wasn't sleepy, which worried him a bit: his muscles weren't secreting the dull, habitual caress of exhaustion. Demetrio suddenly thought of going to see Verónica. He recalled her cheap perfume, their reciprocal sweat; he pictured her low-slung breasts, oscillating like twins in the breeze, her broad hips framing her pale buttocks and concealing the black keyhole of her ass. Sensing a partial erection obstructed by the folds of his pants, he wondered whether he should open the door or turn around and take a bus to Parque Lezama, cross the old tracks, reach the building on Calle Arnaldo d'Espósito, and climb up to the cursed tenth floor where he would meet, once again, his compadre's wife.

But he went home. He shut the door soundlessly, as if the apartment were inhabited by someone he didn't want to wake. He walked past the table without a glance. He looked around for the previous day's paper and sat down on the couch to read it. He learned, vaguely, that the peso had been devalued against the dollar, that Boca was playing in Rosario on Sunday, that the CEOs of an airline still hadn't identified the cause of the catastrophe, that teachers were on hunger strike in Catamarca, that the Argentine president was visiting the United States, that signs pointed to the development of a possible vaccine according to sources of the Research Committee on whatever. He tired quickly, which seemed like a good sign. His eyelids grew heavy and his stomach felt restless. It was nearly noon; he planned to eat whatever he could rustle up and then lie down, sleep until eight o'clock sharp, take a shower, put on his black boots, and work at the table until it was time to go out. He went to the kitchen, imagining a plate of pasta with tomato sauce and a repose full of temperate pleasures, of oblivion.

XXII

The specter of a haunting figure pursued him through fields of amancays and portended storms. But he was the one trailing behind and she the one who was running ahead, luminous in a white nightgown, unattainable as the wind that blustered the sheets into disarray, and even so, yes: she was chasing him.

Long before eight, he lurched out of bed with his forehead drenched in sweat. He fled the room. Standing barefoot in the bathroom, noting a tautness in his pajama pants and hazily remembering some kind of vertigo, he masturbated as if he'd been commanded to. Then the black boots, the paltry dinner, the slow cars through the living room window, the table and the landscape with the turbid sky, and as if building muscle mass, the rocky shoreline of the Perito Moreno or the Nahuel Huapi, a cedar out of place, the pine grove clearer farther out, along the water's edge.

He wonders about the missing myrtles as he shakes the box, stirs shards of sky, grass, water, tree, he feels the smolder as if stewing in a pot and senses that this tiny scrap of ochre is what he's been looking for. He tests it. Little by little, they start to expand across the tabletop: the partial trunks of the forest on Victoria Island, on the banks of the lake, where tourists would flock during the high season to photograph the myrtles' dramatic arc, the frozen time. In the summer, following the fragrance of damp wood, the tourists would throng there and desecrate everything—but in the summer, too, freedom could be reinvented and excursions to the island would begin, accompanied by the figure with the incendiary crest. Perched on logs to talk, playing at smoking. The tourists were led single-file along the least attractive paths as the two of them seized their chance to walk in the opposite direction and lie down together beneath an opulent tree to practice better caresses than the ones available to them in wintertime.

XXIII

The girl was scared, I could see it in her eyes, though her face stayed calm. I still remember how brave I suddenly felt when I noticed her fear. For the first time, she was the one who was afraid, which made me like her more than ever. What do you mean we're going to spend the night here? she said, what will we tell our parents tomorrow? Relax, I answered, it's summer. Reassuring her made me feel like a real man, which is ridiculous, I was two years younger than her.

It was easy to dodge the forest ranger. Euphoric, we saw the last ferryboat set sail, full of homeward travelers. That's when we kissed, and then nothing mattered except for her hands and mine. The woods were cold, her red hair had darkened, I smelled her mane and felt a rush of vertigo like a sweet hangover and bit her hungrily, wearing fewer clothes now, not cold at all. Her breathing reminded me of a downpour falling into the lake or the hum of motorboats setting out with their cargo of washed-up old tourists who would never feel what I was feeling now, never ever. But what am I supposed to tell my parents now, Demetrio. Relax, it's summer, and I held her close.

XXIV

The drenched florescence of their suits parted the curtain of rain. The plastic bags sweated and offered the air some of its stench, which dissolved in the fine torrent coursing through the drains of Calle Piedras. Gleaming, slick, the pavement seemed to yield before the splashes of their rubber boots.

Close to daybreak, soon before they entered the bar on Bolívar that would never be the same again, Demetrio and El Negro looked each other in the eye. Demetrio, who felt the droplets soiling his cheeks and softening his skull, very still, his hair a black pulp, with a weight on his shoulders and his vision diluted, confirmed beyond a shadow of a doubt that El Negro knew nothing, or that he'd never be able to retaliate with hatred. His awkward paw of a hand came to rest fondly on Demetrio's shoulder: he received the stab of this caress as the rain picked up. He patted El Negro on the back, smiling.

Seated at the counter, they stared at the glasses behind the bar, which split the noise in two. Demetrio feared, as he always did in a deluge, that the rain would never stop, that it would pursue him tirelessly and erode his skin and muscles and bones until he disappeared like an old breeze. He felt that the downpour had penned them inside some transparent reserve where they themselves had sought refuge. The coffee cup stuck to his fingers; the hot liquid seared his throat. Casting him a complacent look, El Negro indicated to Demetrio that he would pay, proffering a wet folded bill that the waiter phlegmatically peeled open before he stored it in the cash register and returned with the change. Demetrio advanced toward the exit, imagining that the weight of the water pummeling the door might not let him open it. He suddenly caught a whiff of the house wine, but he couldn't bring himself to turn and glance toward the solitary tables in the corner.

The truck's making a weird noise, Demetrio, don't you think?, in the clutch I mean, not as bad as before they fixed it, but sorta like that, something inside, you know?, like something's come loose, bet they'll tell us at the shop that it's all hunky-dory, just you wait, fuckin idiots, they won't even check till the thing's falling apart, you even listening Demetrio?, in the clutch is what I'm saying. It's like this little noise.

XXV

We escaped to the island three times that summer. I'd pass the time by daydreaming about us making love among the myrtles, slow and tireless. The punishment had been severe; my dad beat the hell out of me. But we escaped together again, and she only had a color and the fragrance of a lake, she'd clutch my arm and believe we were free and her hope made me believe it, too. It was insane that we'd spent the night away from home. More than an adventure, I saw it as a destiny. The third time, though, it rained: hard, really hard, incessant. We huddled together and closed our eyes, not speaking, and the myrtles thrummed and the lake seemed to shatter because of the sky and because of us. And then she kissed me in a different way, a long, sad kiss I didn't fully understand. I felt more passionate than ever that night, and my whole life has been sort of begging for scraps of that feeling ever since. I don't remember if I told her I loved her or what, but I thought about it all night long until I'd convinced myself that there would only be less joy and more fear from then on. When we finally went back on the tourist boat, now carrying fewer tourists in thicker coats, I stepped out onto the shore and saw the muddy path up the hill and felt dead, but powerful.

XXVI

Demetrio raced off the 152 bus and dashed recklessly across Cabildo. He moved away from the traffic and delved into a terrain of darker, tree-sheltered streets. There the passersby were few, well-dressed, their faces serene; some strolled with their dogs. He turned right and studied the opposite sidewalk, looking for a sign. He couldn't find it, grew impatient. Then he turned around and snorted: there it was, right behind him. Before he went into the café, he peered through the window until he spotted Verónica's shiny black hair.

Steam rose from the two cups of coffee, their fragrances mixing at the center of the table. Verónica smoked with mischief. Demetrio sometimes regarded her with tenderness, sometimes avoided her gaze. Her painted lips moved emphatically. That's why I can't do this anymore Demetrio, don't you get it, plus now he's always watching me and expecting me to obey him all the time, I do what I can, you know, sometimes I remember when he and I were dating and wanted to be happy together, like last night, right, I can't even tell you how exhausted I was, running around all day with the house and the kids and school, and then he shows up and after he's done with his nice hot meal and his after-dinner drink and everything he goes and tells me to come to the bedroom, and I'm so tired Demetrio but of course, now Mr. Heartbreak has the right to all his demands, but I can't do it anymore. You have to put up with it just a little longer, love, you know there's nothing else I can do yet, just hang in there a little longer. How am I supposed to hang in there! She glared at him, resentful, chewing at her cigarette smoke. She took two sips of coffee. How am I supposed to do that if we've been carrying on like this forever now. Yeah I know Vero, don't be mad, all I'm saying is be careful. Verónica blew out all the smoke in a single exhalation. Waiter! another coffee for the lady. I don't want more coffee, Demetrio, I want solutions. Okay, one for me then. I need to be brave, not careful! Yes yes of course, what you need is something else. Demetrio squeezed her hand in one of his and placed the other near her thigh. You're a real son of a bitch. And you're a queen, Vero, a queen with the best legs! Get your hand out of there, darling, everyone can see us. Okay Vero but just you wait, you'll see. Demetrio looked at her neck. He loathed these preambles, always conducted in far-flung cafés or some distant park aswarm with children, these cathartic prologues that preceded the real encounter. You look so pretty love, come on, have another coffee and we'll go.

They emerged onto the street, tenuously holding hands. It was drizzling. Two kids darted past. Verónica watched them. Then they walked down Cabildo and turned onto a short, silent street with few doors. Just before the corner, there was a garage and a door set with cloudy glass. Demetrio let Verónica go in first, then sped up to station himself at the front desk. A potbellied man with a thick mustache smiled at them fatuously. Demetrio spoke and the potbelly answered, presenting him with a key. They walked up a couple poorly carpeted flights of stairs and found the number they were looking for at the end of a hallway decorated with knickknacks.

As soon as Demetrio shut the door, he found Verónica exposing her ripened breasts. She used the toes of her bare foot to tug off her other shoe, stepping on the heel. Her skirt fell as if gravity had suddenly begun to act on it. As her stockings curled into themselves like black cream, the hairs on her thighs changed direction. The curt handkerchief concealing her pubis grew wispier and vanished on contact with the rug; her belly shrank and declared itself. Meanwhile, from a slight distance, Demetrio calmly unbuttoned his shirt.

XXVII

Verónica flung him a look charged with intention, far too explicit. Demetrio opened his eyes wider, a warning,. before averting them and asking for a little more salad. The table was laid with oily platters, a demijohn of wine, soda siphons, Coca-Cola, wood-handled cutlery cleaving the meat and making it bleed its crimson juice, and bread in abundance, shredded and scattered into numberless bits around the plates; all atop an old white-and-blue checkered canvas tablecloth.

Demetrio avoided Verónica's gaze and focused instead on the two boys, who shrieked with bliss between mouthfuls. The older one had bangs that curtained his eyelids. He wrinkled his nose as he spoke, flashing a gap in his smile, while the younger one interrupted incessantly and cackled with his head thrown back, releasing a sharp, intermittent noise that set Demetrio's nerves on edge, although it also stirred some long-secluded paternal sentiment deep inside him. They knew his name and pronounced it comfortably when they greeted him, extending ceremonious hands just as their father had taught them men greet each other. Their father, El Negro, who clapped Demetrio affectionately on the back and refilled his glass, who occasionally enveloped his wife in protective, energetic arms, who beheld the vivacity of his filial sprouts, the light in his eyes conferred both by fatherly pride and especially by alcohol; El Negro, thought Demetrio, who was surely the happiest cuckold on earth.

Accepting the invitation had required less cold blood than sheer negligence. It was the first time they'd all shared a meal since Demetrio had started sleeping with Verónica, or at least since he'd started doing so often; entire months when the fissure between work and pleasure had exempted him from harsher trials of conscience. But now the challenge was to behave naturally while confronting their simultaneous presence, and Demetrio was struggling, less because of guilt—time had eased that long ago—but because he felt awkward that El Negro, affable and pathetic behind his moustache and swollen belly, was so blind. And so Demetrio occupied himself with the spectacle of the two kids, concentrating on their eyes, eager to take it all in, trying to absorb their innocence. More wine, Demetrio? It's good shit this red.

The second glance was fleeting but decisive. Demetrio understood that he'd have to act fast if he wanted to put an end to the game, and he didn't hesitate before picking up his plate and walking toward the kitchen, where Verónica had just disappeared. El Negro stayed at the table, making a racket with his children, and their voices instantly dimmed behind the door. She awaited him with blazing eyes and the tip of her tongue gleaming between her teeth. Keeping calm, confirming that the uproar in the dining room was still composed of three voices, Demetrio threw himself onto Verónica, finding her breasts.

XXVIII

His mind was blank when he got home. He felt the weight of alcohol, fatigue, and rage. He stood at the toilet bowl and observed his reflection before the stream of urine diluted his face.

He woke around eight and wandered the apartment in search of an appetite. Weary of waiting, he stopped at the window, his pupils tinged by the fluorescent glow of closing storefronts. The traffic on Federico Lacroze dispersed and dissolved into the darkness. His eyes followed several passersby until he lost them at the corner of the train station. They never acknowledged each other as they walked. Demetrio suddenly longed to go downstairs and speak to them, then hear his own name called from a window by someone who, peering out from above, was addressing a passerby like him, and greet that someone, and ask them to come down.

He returned to the living room and glanced at his watch. He noted that he still wasn't hungry and decided to skip dinner. Yawning, already glimpsing the night's lucidity as it approached, he sat at the table and picked up a handful of pieces. He saw the pine grove near-complete, sharp-edged and misted by the shore, a pair of cedar trees that flanked the path down to the rocks. Like a punctilious scroll, the amancay appeared to fracture in the face of the advancing storm, delivering each leaf into the squall. The hills and foam evoked the chaos, but the most important part was missing. Demetrio rummaged in the box, which contained just a few pieces now. The spectral, haunting figure was gone.

They'd agreed about the risks of desiring each other. They were united by the ambiguous bond of carnal awakening. He remembered the kiss they'd shared before each vanished along a different fork of the muddy path. For him, it had been the irrevocable kiss of a boy accepting his punishment. Her eyes, though, and her final kiss, hadn't been so certain; fear seemed stronger than euphoria. When he found himself alone, following the path toward the cabin, he thought for the first time since they'd left for the island that their audacity may have been a mistake. Facing the house, it was his father who heard his footsteps first, or who sensed his return with the olfaction of authority defied. He was waiting, standing in the doorway, a long stick in his hands.

A couple housebound months. At night, the creaking floorboards kept him awake, though he rarely felt like sleeping. During the day, the cabin was all sticky heat and reverberating birds. It was then, barred from chasing cats or inhaling the breath of the lake, that he embarked on the final cause of his insomnia: on top of a wardrobe he found two old, five-hundred-piece puzzles, dust-coated and slightly damp, to which he surrendered in hopes of exhausting himself and finally being able to forget the figure with the twilight tangled in her hair.

XXIX

On that harsh and cloudy morning, Demetrio had witnessed two events that finally convinced him he didn't belong to the city, that he was incorrigibly foreign to the afflictions of countless pedestrians, drivers, vendors, beggars, police officers, prostitutes, students. He and El Negro had begun their pickup punctually at the start of Avenida Independencia. The icy wind seeping in from the port didn't blow as it did most days; it stumbled obstinately into things, making the street lurch and stagger instead of shaking it with a single gust; and so it seeped, too, into their neon suits, circulating in every interstice, infiltrating through their wrists and ankles.

The collection had carried on monotonously and in silence until five, when Demetrio, seated at the wheel as El Negro loaded the bags into the back, noticed two men fiddling nervously outside a gray Ford Falcon. The scene was unfolding across the street and El Negro couldn't see it, but Demetrio had a perfect panoramic view from his perch: one of the guys was standing in front, covering his counterpart, who struggled clumsily to jimmy the lock and get into the vehicle, where he fumbled for maybe thirty seconds before signaling for his companion to follow. Demetrio realized then that he should have alerted El Negro or gotten out himself, or that he should at least cross the street now that the car hadn't yet revved into motion and try to halt their escape. But he did none of this, nor did he venture even the slightest movement as he observed the brusque jounces of the Ford, which finally vanished up the street. Demetrio knew exactly what he was supposed to do: take down the license plate number, which he'd effortlessly memorized, and report the theft to the police. Just a few meters away, in fact, just before Calle Defensa, was the San Telmo precinct. In an involuntary evocation, he discovered that he remembered the first man's face, build, and even his attire in perfect detail; somewhat more vaguely, he recalled the second man's appearance and jacket. But Demetrio showed no signs of getting out of the truck. And when El Negro finally got in on the passenger side, he didn't feel like telling him what he'd seen.

The second event occurred when they were about to finish their route. The light, heavy and lazy, had begun to stain the buildings. A young student, maybe fifteen years old, one of those girls who could be mistaken for a woman if it weren't for a sort of cheerful unease in her movements, had walked by with a folder clutched to her chest. While El

Negro was busy with the bags, Demetrio saw a man emerge from a doorway and trail her from close behind. After staring fixedly and obviously at her legs, the man drew himself right up to her and whispered something into her ear. Demetrio saw that everything was happening with obnoxious clarity: the student's body went stiff and she moved forward very slowly, chin held high; suddenly they both turned and retraced, the man grabbing her around the waist and the girl arching her back, trying to avoid the touch of what was likely a razor. That was when a distant voice sounded in Demetrio's mind as he watched through the window. And that voice grew louder and more meaningful and arranged itself into something like a scream of alarm when El Negro, sweaty, got into the truck and said let's go come on, what are you waiting for, step on it.

Demetrio would spend days and weeks repeating to himself that it hadn't been him, not exactly him, just his hands and his feet, thoughtless, mechanical, that had turned the key in the ignition and drove off quickly so they wouldn't miss the green light.

XXX

The first week I was grounded put me to rights. I was sort of crazed at first, and the peace of the cabin calmed me down, boring as it was. The real trouble began when the silence grew unbearable, and the heat of the wood started to remind me that it was still summer outside and the sun hadn't stopped heating the shore. When I realized, in short, that I was alone.

I'd never been able to sleep like my old man, who, as soon as he hit the mattress, assuming he didn't first do the deed with my mom, which was rare, would conk out and sleep like a log for seven hours straight. I got almost all of his worst qualities, but in this way I turned out more like my grandfather Jacinto, who apparently lived out his final days raving with insomnia. I'd never slept well, but those two months left a permanent hollow under my eyes. I'd try to recharge by napping after my mother's lunches—as calorie-packed in the summer as they were in the cold months—when I'd be flooded with a kind of sweet drowsiness. But then I'd wake up two, three hours later, and stay up for the rest of the evening and almost all night, with just a couple intervals of sleep that would be instantly broken by some thought or sudden fear.

That's when the problems began, not to mention the bad solutions. And the puzzles. I put a few together when I was little, but I'd always found it incredibly stupid: spending so many hours reconstructing a photo that was already complete on the cover, instead of going out to play hide-and-seek or tease the cats. But that's just if you don't have enough hours, if you feel like time is a party you'd better crash before it's over. If it feels like the hours don't pass at all, like it's never the last night but always the same, the first, the only night ever, then finding something to do, especially something that gives you a sense of order, is nothing short of salvation from madness . . .

(Demetrio confirmed that the storm was reaching completion, that the prowling veil had cohered and was gradually encroaching into the pines on the left side and above the faded horizon. The araucarias, candelabra of rage; an amancay disfigured by wind—it all convened in an image identical to the photo on the box. The cabin wasn't pictured there, but he remembered it, could visualize it as neatly as the radiant neons on the street that tinted his windowpane.)

I thought of her during the night. Working at the table in my room, with a little lamp that cast an ugly, yellowish glow, my thoughts would sometimes drift back to Victoria

Island, to the myrtles, to the deep black earth. I tried to keep myself from doing it, stop thinking, don't even try, but in the end some little drowsy nod of the head would bring the island up to the table or drag my bedroom out to the lake, and then I'd try to imagine a photo that was almost like the memory of what I'd dreamed, and everything would relocate there, to the image on the table. I don't know. All I know is that it was around then that the problems really began.

XXXI

Two coffees, kid. And no rush cause we got time today. El
Negro spoke with an air of self-sufficiency that Demetrio
knew well and found particularly irritating at six-thirty in
the morning. El Negro turned and winked at him, and
Demetrio responded with a vacant gaze in lieu of a more
vehement sneer, a scorn inherent to a later hour. Just look
at you, he thought, all slow on the uptake, winking like
an idiot. Then his attention drifted into the empty corner
where the Pony used to sit; he noticed that one of the tables
had no chairs and sported a dried rose resting diagonally
across the surface.

It was almost nine. Exhausted, full of minuscule tremors
rising into his muscles, Demetrio tried to breathe amid the
glancing contact of other people's clothes and limbs on the
93 bus. Through the window, he watched Plaza Francia
whisk past, brimming with green, waiting for children and
the weekend to climb aboard, and then the cement barrier

around the Recoleta cemetery, that empire that safeguarded the famous dead but never men like him, whose bones would be laid instead into the old soil of Chacarita or in some niche with an illegible plaque. In other words I'll rest where I rest, I'll be dead where I live now, holy smokes. And with this thought his eyes cleared.

Federico Lacroze felt like it was about to be transformed into a petrified forest. Every scene stretched out longer than necessary, pedestrians took forever to cross the street, flowers of slowness bloomed up from the subway; vendors of candied nuts and lighters and pens called out their wares; their shouts kept sounding from the corners; the buses froze in Chacarita and never pitched forward again. Demetrio struggled down the street toward home.

When he finally reached the door to his apartment and pulled it shut behind him, things regained their normal speed; he even managed to shower with a suspicious glimmer of cheer. He read the newspaper in rigorous disarray. He made a salad with cold rice, boiled egg, and sliced tomato, then a heavily salted veal filet. He poured himself what was left of the wine and devoured his food with the euphoria of the starved. Once finished, he sat on the living room couch with a bottle of grappa and a thick glass between his knees. He took quick, eager gulps until the house felt strange and alive and he could sense the garbage disposal in the distance, superimposing itself over the muffled voice of El Negro as he argued with Verónica, and his own breath smelled like myrtle. He set the bottle on the floor. He groped clumsily for the sheets. He dreamed of something monstrous. He woke at eight, amnesiac.

XXXII

Panting into his neck, pulling on his hair, lacing her legs around his back, pressing her belly into Demetrio's, Verónica rose up in a final arch and then plummeted as if disassembled. Soon they were both groaning again, this time without looking each other in the eye, she sinking her knees and hands into the sheets, he gripping her from behind, coming and going. There was a moment of blindness, of disorientation with every movement, and then their mingled sweat in abrupt repose.

Verónica lit a cigarette and stretched out on her back, looking up at the ceiling, at the invisible horizon that only sated lovers can see. They lay there in silence for a while, until she spoke. You're killing me Demetrio, you have to do something. And he did: he flung himself onto her, yanked her arms above her head, and gripped her hard. Pulling free and straddling him now, imprisoning him between her thighs, Verónica slapped Demetrio, enraged.

XXXIII

The coats roaming Calle Corrientes were getting finer. The restaurants were filling up, the movie theaters had reupholstered their seats, the twenty-four-hour convenience stores had never before gleamed so brightly or seemed so bilingual. Certainly, particular details of the landscape were being extinguished: small cinemas with different titles; dusty secondhand bookstores with their scent of singed pages, staffed by improbably old men who knew everything by heart; more modestly furnished cafés. And still, what radiance in these passersby: Demetrio watched them earnestly emerge from taxis, exuding cologne. Demetrio, who seldom came downtown, was struck by the change without worrying about it.

He took Reconquista to Lavalle, which reared up before him like a two-hued creature, a large bicephalous tiger: on one side ran stripes enveloped in leather, jewels, hides; on the other, rope after rope strung with dirty silhouettes. Their paths occasionally crossed, and then he heard a refusal, an insistence, a brusque acceleration in the click-clacking of shoes. This music wasn't foreign to Demetrio, but it seemed more frequent now. He stepped laboriously between the two rows, gold and gray, noting a suffocating pressure on both sides.

He glimpsed the window display of a toy store and slipped through the crowd. It exhibited dolls, balls, fortresses, miniature houses, strange space weapons, light-flashing objects of uncertain purpose—nothing that interested him. He went in and asked the clerk, who looked at him, perplexed, and said no.

He paid fruitless visits to several more toy stores. Some didn't even sell five-hundred-piece puzzles. And those that did had none depicting any photos of Bariloche, of its mountains, lakes, and flora.

Demetrio retraced Lavalle, foul-tempered. Dusk fell slowly and the lingering August chill seemed reluctant to leave the city. He was walking toward the 93 bus stop when, suddenly, a timid glimmer interrupted his path. He stopped in front of a dimly lit window display. He took a few steps; drawing his nose close to the glass, and immediately noticed the box he'd been looking for. He burst into the store, asked for the box without any other questions, paid, left, and fled from the city center, clutching five hundred seeds of an alpine inn with views of the Nahuel Huapi under his arm.

XXXIV

Cold Spanish omelet; reheated veal; bad wine; and a listlessly peeled orange. Then copious coffee to clear his head. As he showered, Demetrio examined his body and determined that his belly was of reasonable size, his legs were still firm, his member didn't look too worn-out. The hair on his chest remained quite dark and the volume of hair that collected in the shower grate wasn't too alarming yet. He felt almost good when he shut off the water. His skin beaded freshly and the towel rubbed him dry with a friendly touch. He put on a checkered shirt, a pair of jeans, and the old black boots that awaited him at the foot of the bed. He went to the living room and sat, without stopping by the window, at the table, where everything was ready.

The chimney appeared first. It came out of nowhere, close to the upper edge, like a bird of smoke tilting its curious head. Then it was easier to move on to the roof, elucidating its isosceles profile, the speck of foliage behind it; next, the solid mass of beams, the shimmer on the glass of what would become a window, and then, almost, the stead-fast purr of the current and the tender breeze . . .

Who knows why troubles seek each other out as if trying to start a family, but everything jumbled together that summer. From my room, I could hear the Nahuel flowing differently, hurrying, far too restless for January. Housebound as I was, I couldn't really make sense of how things were going outside, but there was a certain advantage to being cooped up: I got to hear my old man talking. Over the course of those two months, through the same walls that had let me know my parents still occasionally desired each other, I would overhear the news that my dad brought back from the slaughterhouse, though his voice would drop lower and lower. The last words were pretty much inaudible.

(And emphasized, alone, the awe-inspiring trunk of a protective cedar. The turquoise of the sky around the smoke can only indicate midday. As if by chance, white blossoms float around the fragment like a golden eye, and then an archipelago of tall, unruly glass, and coins of water here and there, dispersed.)

At night, I no longer heard the groan of the springs in their cots, just their voices: my old man's, constant, fierce; and my mom's, anxious and sporadic. Things kept getting worse and worse: production plummeted, and rumor had it that the slaughterhouse would be downsized, even shut down altogether. But my old man kept getting up with the sun, eating his breakfast slowly, and my mom accompanied him in silence, not eating a thing, and she kept bringing him his lunch in a plastic box and returning by dusk, when the cold loosened the wood and the cabin began to creak. Meanwhile, I'd stopped even trying to sleep, resigning myself to exhaustion. Sometimes, at the hour of the strange birds and the moon's last reflection on the Nahuel, the girl would appear before me, floating in the window or on the tabletop.

XXXV

At the end of the day, work's the most important thing you know, cause it's not your Sunday nap or the game or your family that puts food on the table, and anyway those are the first mouths you gotta feed, amirite? That's what I always said to Demetrio but he seemed off, we weren't talking much cause he was I don't know, off. I'd tell him, look bro if you start showing up late and this is how you're gonna work, like not even trying, then we're fucked, but I never got a word out of him, what can you do. Of course I say to him you don't have kids, you can afford to say you're fuckin sick of bagging trash, you really think I like it, kid? But you're old, he says to me, and we both crack up, you're old, he says to me, and I say to him, no, Demetrio, I just learned to deal.

Sometimes I say to my wife, I tell her I think Demetrio's up to something weird. Weird how? she says and I say I don't know but it's weird. She couldn't see it but she heard me out, I had her on a real tight leash for months after all that bullshit that happened, I forgave her cause you gotta be a good Christian in this life and besides no one else found out and it was just once, she swore, crying she swore it, just once and that was it. You know who I think the other guy was, it was that sonofabitch from the third floor, you know the guy I mean?, I caught the motherfucker giving Verónica the once-over a few times, if I make sure it was him I'm gonna bust down his door and kick the shit out of him, she swore it wasn't, not him, let's forget it ever happened, she says. But anyway, she hears me out and she says Negro don't waste your breath on Demetrio, he was never a hardworking guy like you Negrito, he's always tired and he lives alone, can't you see he doesn't have anyone to talk to, he must be lonely. And it's true, she was right, Verónica, because at the end of the day at least you got a wife that loves you and a couple healthy kids that're getting an education thank god.

That's why I had him over for lunch some Saturdays, you know, so he wouldn't stay cooped up all alone all day, and at first yeah he came over and we had a grand old time drinking wine and talking about soccer. But then he started coming less, he was always busy, he had to do this or that or whatever on Saturday, what do I know. So obviously yeah we stopped calling him and things sort of petered out after that. This one time I even had a fight with Verónica because she was kind of rude to him and I said to her is this how you're gonna treat a guest, I can't fuckin believe it. Maybe he got offended, pff, I mean I don't think so, but then he stopped coming over out of the blue. Yeah well he was always a little like that anyway, you know?, like in and out. Sometimes breakfast was on me, just like a nice thing to do for your buddy, you know, cause he seemed all down in the mouth lately, but then I remember how one day he goes and says to me you're an idiot Negro, on top of everything you buy me breakfast, and I started cracking up but he stayed all serious. Kinda weird.

XXXVI

Just before Avenida Independencia drains out into the brutal artery, into the mass grave of 9 de Julio, is Calle Tacuarí. Modest and sparsely trafficked, Tacuarí was the site of their last collection stops. Demetrio and El Negro appreciated this street because it extended all the way down to Avenida San Juan, where they could park by the intersection with Bolívar and have breakfast before making their way back to the dump. The viscous light from the streetlamps clung to the corners of the streets called Venezuela, México, Chile. The two silhouettes catalogued them laboriously. Apathetic, Demetrio handed El Negro the bags in a way that seemed to emphasize their contents. El Negro received them, murmuring. They'd just finished one side of Tacuarí and were getting back into the truck to take care of the other side when Demetrio suddenly noticed a gray bulge and a silvery beard in the shadows of a doorway. He pointed out the sight to El Negro, who was equally puzzled: they knew every street by heart, every cat and thief and beggar. They'd never seen this one before.

Feeling watched, the old man—who wasn't sleeping at all—moaned a splintery phrase and slowly peeked his nose out into the grayish light. El Negro crouched down as the nose grew closer, until they were nearly face-to-face: it was a bulbous, warty nose planted above a moustache that blurred into a shapeless beard. A small, dark-lipped mouth shone through an orifice in all the hair. The mouth spoke, and it told them to go jump in a lake. Abruptly entertained, Demetrio explained that they didn't mean to bother him, but they'd never seen him there before and found it odd. The beggar, revealing a pair of shifty eyes and a crooked hat, confirmed that it was only the second night he'd spent on that street and launched into a monologue. Demetrio and El Negro learned then that he'd shared a campfire with the ragtag crew on 9 de Julio, but they were a tyrannical lot and tended to form gangs that disputed territory and cast-offs, cracking down on the weakest vagrants or gangless loners, like him, who was too old to defend his authority and too experienced to tolerate taking orders. So he'd decided to move to Calle Tacuarí, no man's land, where he hoped he'd sleep better and maybe even encounter some charity, or at least some halfway decent garbage. Demetrio, listening, was flooded with inexplicable joy. Despite El Negro's bewilderment and protestations, he invited the old man to get into the truck with them, addressing him formally and opening the door so he could step up first.

The old man, it must be said, didn't exactly smell like

roses: his coat gave off dust condensed by humidity, the whitish ash exhaled by the mouth of time. His hat, once made of felt, infused his matted hair with the stench of old rope. His fingers were long and grimy, blackened phalanges that touched everything with empty-handed gusto. And El Negro wasn't thrilled about any of it. But there was something about the eyes of the old Tacuarí beggar, something about his gaze as he contemplated the streets from the truck, a certain amnesiac, childlike happiness, that filled Demetrio's morning to the brim.

The waiter at the bar on Bolívar was baffled by the procession: El Negro in the lead, imposing, heavily mustached, exuding irritation, encased in his neon suit, followed by a more cheerful Demetrio in identical attire, delicately taking the forearm of a shabby, ratty, elderly man who insisted he could walk on his own two feet. They settled in at the counter and ordered three cafés con leche and three medialunas. The old Tacuarí beggar regarded the cup set down in front of him, then looked at Demetrio and smiled a meager-toothed smile. Undertaking a leisurely rite of dissection, he lifted the medialuna to his mouth in pieces, then downed his coffee in a single gulp and a brusque tracheal jerk. Instead of adding sugar to his coffee, Demetrio noticed, he slipped the packet into his pocket, along with the spoon. Demetrio asked the waiter to charge him for all of it. El Negro looked uneasy. The old Tacuarí beggar dug a hand into his coat and extracted a small tin can he shook like a rattle. He held it out to Demetrio, who refused it, laughing: please, don't even think about it. The old man shrugged, thanked him with no further fuss, and tucked the can away again.

They returned to the truck. Demetrio invited him to get back in and told him where they were going, describing the garbage dump as if it were a toy store. The old man's button-eyes lit up for an instant, but then he seemed frightened; he was worried he'd be tired out by such a long trip, he explained, and preferred to return to Tacuarí. Demetrio offered to drop him off at the doorway. The old Tacuarí beggar thanked him and insisted there was no need: a brief walk every morning was good for the bones.

XXXVII

The smoke tangled like a transparent vine. When they blew, the curls threatened to flee, then coalesced into a pillar that continued its impassive ascent.

Verónica's cigarette, which peeked its incandescent head through her fingers as if probing between two legs, was nearly spent. They were naked. Lying on their backs, studying the part of the ceiling accentuated by the light, they didn't look at each other. Their voices couldn't be heard. They breathed to the rhythm of the smoke.

The room revealed a chair beside the bed, with men's clothing folded over the back, and, deeper in, some curtains tinged with the street's anemic glow. Everything else was shrouded in shadow, except for a woman's shoe and a scrap of carpet underscored by a beam slipping in under the door.

Demetrio started to think about the time, about how Verónica's children would soon be leaving their little friend's birthday party, about how he felt like working on his puzzles at home instead of lying buck-naked in a hotel and in silence. You should probably get going, he said more coldly than he'd expected, or you'll be late. She seemed to postpone her reply until the final drag; exhaling the smoke, she watched it disappear and unstuck her lips with a faint snap. I know, they're my kids in case you forgot.

Verónica turned toward the nightstand and crushed the cigarette into the glass ashtray, the bottom engraved with a medieval emblem. Well I'm going to get dressed, Demetrio murmured, not yet moving. It's half past, she replied, I have plenty of time if I take a cab, why don't you come a little closer and we can stay ten more minutes, who cares anyway. Yeah Vero but I don't know what's the point of waiting till the last minute if you already know what's next, the nerves, the racing around, it's always the same. Okay, but maybe the thing for me is we don't get to see each other much and I like to make the most of it, so I care more about that than the nerves and the racing around all put together, you get it? Look Vero what can I say, I don't know if staying a few more minutes when you know you have to go and grab a taxi is really making the most of it, and about how we don't see each other much, I mean that depends. Well I'll be damned, it's funny that this never comes up when your dick's doing the talking. And what would happen if I said it? You're not man enough for that. Maybe your husband's man enough, but then I wouldn't know what you're cheating on him with me for. You're a real fucking son of a bitch, Demetrio. You're going to be late, come on love.

XXXVIII

There were nights when I was consumed with anxiety but couldn't even jack off in the bathroom when I went, it was a mix of nausea and fear, sometimes I thought I heard the redhead's voice among the myrtles and I'd cry myself breathless. At least then I could get some sleep. Then the same breakfast every morning, my old man had already left for the slaughterhouse, my mom and I would eat stale bread and homemade jam. At some point she'd look at me and then start crying too and say she'd been thinking about my brother Martín, who was doing his military service in Neuquén, and she knew he'd never live with us again and in a couple more years it would be my turn, and please could I come back to help my old man because things were getting worse and worse. But I couldn't console her, much less cry with her; it was all I could do to feel even a little bit moved by her surge of feeling. I'd already used up all my tears the night before.

(On every windowsill are flowering plants that look like flags. No one peers out for a glimpse of the sentinel cedar whose trunk shrinks squat, or at the fragments—isolated, though familiar now—of the lake's mirror. The pathway's ochre tongue still hasn't shown its end. It may not have one. The chalkboard of the roof, a stubborn night at noon, keeps soaking up the shine of an anarchic sun, invisible for now.)

I wasn't really sure, but one cool evening I knew. Dad arrived home too affectionate, more than he'd ever been. We ate dinner in silence and every so often he'd glance at me and smile in a way I found alarming, as if he pitied me for something that hadn't happened yet. They sent me straight to my room without even asking me to clear the table or wash the dishes, so I shut the door and set out to finish a jigsaw puzzle. The next day, my mom explained, looking weary, that when autumn came I wouldn't be able to go back to school like I did every year, and she hugged me and whispered into my ear that I'd have to grow up fast.

XXXIX

El Negro's voluminous silhouette rested like any other protuberance in the dark. The garbage trucks slept a heavy sleep, cooling their stomachs. As he walked, Demetrio stared so intently at El Negro that he forgot which body was the one in motion: he had the sensation that it was he himself, paralyzed, who was watching El Negro swell in size and advance toward him, who awaited warily, ready for anything.

From his location in the garage, though, El Negro didn't even notice Demetrio until quite late, when his face gleamed forth in the glow of the bulbs at the entrance. El Negro had already sheathed himself in his neon suit and yawned, tugging on his mustache, ostensibly scratching a testicle as a man only does when he thinks he's alone. From the guard's booth came the weepy bellow of the bandonion and an anguished voice whispering a tango, like an echo or a memory. Only when they found themselves face to face did Demetrio say hey Negro what's up, as if he wanted to have him square in his sights to observe his reaction, another day another dollar man, his partner said, releasing a formidable yawn that made his whiskers tremble. Demetrio relaxed.

The traffic light issued its red warning to no one. They didn't generally pay much attention to the stoplights until later on, when the traffic picked up, but Demetrio kept staring at this one, his hands motionless on the wheel. He stayed frozen there until the incandescence dropped and changed color like a checker on a board, and then he sat up straight in his seat and said, know what, let's go see the old guy. El Negro simply crossed his arms and looked at Demetrio, waiting for an explanation. But the truck soon braked on the corner of Independencia and Tacuarí. Only Demetrio got out and headed for the second doorway on the right. He didn't see anyone at first, and he was worried, but then he moved on to the next one and there—curled against the frame, balanced on the stoop, his head so thoroughly concealed by his lapel that he looked like a mere coat discarded in the threshold with a hat on top—he was. Demetrio issued a loud *ahem*. A tremor rose from the folds of the coat, and, like a chelonian emerging from the muck, the old man's salt-and-pepper mane and large, pocked nose appeared.

Noting that Demetrio was taking longer than usual, El Negro got out of the truck to remind him how behind schedule they were. He approached, saw the other two heading his way, and turned exasperated on his heel. The three men converged at the corner. The beggar climbed fluidly into the truck and settled into the middle of the front seat.

Demetrio took his place at the wheel. But El Negro didn't get in. He stood stock-still beside the door, staring at them, hands on his hips. What's wrong, isn't he coming? the old man asked, trying to straighten his hat.

XL

It was mostly glass and plastic at that hour. Cans would predominate later in the day, then glass again, around dusk, which Demetrio was never around to see. Now he beheld the glittering of the glassy shards, the dented empty drums like islets that had survived some filthy and methodical flood. He wasn't sure what happened to it all over the years, where the excess of the mountainous dump would go, into what stomach or what mouth. It was logical, inevitable, that the heap would grow, but the dump was now so vast, its gluttony so absolute, that it looked impossible to fill: its volume never seemed to change.

He imagined that the mass, once it had digested its putrid daily feast, would excrete the leftovers toward the heart of the city, where they would disperse and make their way into every home, and into those containers on the street that would later feed the dump once more, and so on, over and over again. It was interesting, the question of shit and its itinerary. Maybe not as interesting as movies or soccer, or bars. But I'm not an actor or a soccer player or a bartender either, thought Demetrio, I'm a garbage collector and I should think about the shit I work with. He actually wasn't bothered by the idea of staring at all this stuff every morning of his life; all he had to do was stay as he was, exactly as he was. A cloud shifted overhead and the bottles lit up in the sun, bleak as flashlights after a battle.

XLI

Look I never liked that bum and I told him so okay, I don't know why the fuck we're gonna drive him around like he's a count or something, we're working hard here and then he gets all excited over some filthy hobo, Jesus Christ. Anyway at least now I know why Demetrio was doing all that shit, I mean, I don't know if I *know* but one day I said chau!, right, I get it, I think he did that kind of stuff so he wouldn't have to think too much.

He seemed kind of lost, we weren't talking a lot, like I said, but it was one of two things with the guy, either he'd be wracking his brains over something and making faces all morning or out of the blue he'd cheer up over some bullshit like that, like the thing with the hobo. Can't you see that we're dead Negro, he says to me, and you accept it. And what about you, I say back, you think you don't accept it too? No, I don't accept it, he says, I resign myself.

So yeah, it was weird. Right when he said that and he seemed like he was doing better, a little later, maybe a month later, I don't know, right after the thing with the hobo the other thing happened. And I know it hurt him, it was like a betrayal or something, but you know after that he started complaining less and doing good work, quiet but good, and at first I thought: finally the guy's decided to chill the fuck out, no more bullshit from now on. And I was glad about it, you know! I was really glad. But then it turns out no, it was the other way around. The thing is he didn't even have the words for how bad off he was.

XLII

Dad got compensation from the slaughterhouse. Not much cash, but enough to bum around for a while. As in, it wasn't just the money problem that made him sick. I watched how my mom watched him, and it was obvious that something wasn't right, would never be right again, it was terrible to see my old man stuck in the dining room for so many months, first at the window, peeking out at the sort of tired-looking happiness of the amancay trees, then staring down at the carpet of dry leaves on the grass, then sitting in front of the fireplace, piled higher and higher with wood, and he'd keep sitting there with a blanket tucked over his legs, terrible to see the months aging his face by years without thinking that something had to change.

He either didn't look for work or didn't know how to find it, I can't remember which. I do know that my mom was obsessed with saving money and I wasn't really sure what for. My old man got up only once on an evening with weak light, I do remember that. I could hear shouting like before, my mom's voice trying to soothe him and my dad's roar filling the whole house again, then the creak of their bed springs. My mom had talked about finding a job herself. He hadn't reacted right away, he'd listened during dinner without a word, absent, then went to sit in front of the fire, looking like he was about to take a nap, but suddenly he leapt up like a furious animal and lit into her, how could she think of doing such a thing, there were solutions that weren't solutions because they insulted a man's dignity, they hadn't run out of money yet, if we wanted to make him so mad it killed him then we were on the right track. In the end, that phrase was like a bullet my dad fired through his own temple, but it passed through my mom's, too, and it's been traveling toward my own ever since. I always thought: at least I managed to dodge the shot. But shit, now I wonder if that bullet had killed me first and I hadn't even noticed, like what happened with their savings, I always caught on too late.

That night the yelling stopped, it was the last time I'd ever hear yelling at home and the first time I really doubted who was taking care of who, if we really were a family at all, or if maybe I was the orphaned son of two orphaned parents, if my life from then on wouldn't always be full of fucked-up questions like that.

XLIII

Exhausted, unmoved before the possible beauties of the sky ablaze, standing at the edge of the great pit, Demetrio thought of the old Tacuarí beggar. He'd refused once again to accompany them to the garage that day. The cold, his bones, his fear of distance, his age, all the most reasonable motives abruptly crumbled before a single certitude: it was the old man's dignity that kept him from coming. As if the chance to visit a fetid place where he could find infinite quantities of what he struggled to obtain from garbage cans and the street were so tempting that it humiliated him.

Demetrio had parted ways with El Negro a few minutes back. He'd watched him fade away down the hill, like every other day, growing rounder and rounder, less and less alert, stupidly flapping his hand goodbye to Demetrio, who stood immobile beside the hole. He went into the garage to change his clothes and leave his uniform inside the truck. Soon after, he awaited the unpredictable arrival of the 93 bus, getting in line by the post office. Demetrio was too far back in the queue to secure a place for himself among the chosen when the vehicle pulled in, chockablock, shuddering.

Did the old Tacuarí beggar use public transit? Demetrio tried to imagine what life would be like if lived entirely on foot, entirely houseless. Although, he reasoned, even if the old man ate only scraps, he'd never had to spend his days carting them around. What would it be like to live among waste, to be another piece of it?

XLIV

This is what Demetrio dreamed one viscous, cast-off evening.

He slips down the street, which is nameless but familiar. Flat figures pass him by, people made of clipped newspaper, lured by some magnetic source that lies behind Demetrio, the only one walking in the other direction. He hears the passersby rush down the road, but he can only see them for a fraction of a second. Unruffled by all of this, he keeps advancing along the avenue, so it's an avenue, then. One he knows well. Suddenly he finds himself on the verge of walking into a bar, but he doesn't recognize either the neighborhood or the street, not even the door of the bar. He decides not to go in and walks away. He rounds curves that aren't exactly new to him, suspecting that he's looped back to where he started, but then he thinks maybe he's just remembering his earlier route as he walks down another similar avenue, although he's not sure where the beginning was, either. His footsteps aren't normal; sometimes they feel very short and sometimes it's like he's taking hugely disproportionate strides. Reaching an intersection where many narrow streets splay out like the spokes of a bicycle wheel, he stops and suffers. He suspects, or feels, or knows he won't be able to decide. He breaks into silent, almost indifferent tears. Then, from one of the little lanes that come and go, a short, bow-legged man appears, wearing an old engine-driver's cap, and it's none other than the Pony, or at least someone who looks exactly like the Pony. For a moment, Demetrio fears he won't recognize him, that he'll rush on like the newspaper-print pedestrians, but the Pony doesn't only recognize him, he hugs him—as best he can, tiny as he is—with jubilant fondness. Demetrio accepts and returns this affection and pays for the Pony's glass of wine. Then they get up from their seats at the bar and emerge onto the first avenue, beside a cemetery that overlooks a lake. Demetrio suddenly finds himself alone, and silhouettes, volatile, multiplying, pass him on both sides. He starts to count them. When he's done counting, the intersection that looks like the hub of a bicycle wheel is far smaller than it had seemed at first, and Demetrio fairly quickly locates the doorway he's looking for: it's that one, it's that one, the Pony, who is now back, points out, pedaling. The Pony says something and instantly disappears again, though not for long, because Demetrio has chosen a door and approaches the dark lump huddled in the threshold, seizing its hat and yanking off its coat, which frays and unravels entirely, just like a ball of wool: it's the Pony, hatless and coatless and naked, covering his face with a mischievous look and exclaiming from his stoop: you found me! And he doesn't have any teeth or gums in his mouth, just a gaping black hole. Demetrio then wonders whether he's still standing there or lying between sheets that could use a good wash.

XLV

I think maybe you start a family to kill off the orphaned feeling you've had since you were born. That's the sensation I always had when I saw my mom bringing soup and bread to my old man and he wouldn't even look at her, just kept focusing on the fireplace, as if imagining his own pyre, trying to get used to the flames. We all felt alone when we were together.

(Now then. The cedar is in charge, the sovereign of the grove. If it could shoot up any faster, it would kill the birds that cut across the sky. The image is precise. The pathway's dusty tongue comes to its end, grazes the shore. As for the water, motionless, its unfoamed face is slumbering, missing two scraps. Demetrio knows which. Atop the table in an almost-empty box, the fragments tumble, flashes of a flame that knows how little it's got left.)

We didn't have leftover anything, not even firewood. Early that winter, we'd filled the shed, but Dad had to start making do with little, and he'd shuffle his legs under the wool blanket to keep himself warm. You enjoy your life now, he'd say to me. Live. He'd ungrounded me the week before, so I could breathe in the air of the Nahuel again. Go on, come home early but do whatever you want, you're all grown up now anyway, aren't you? Suddenly my old man was speaking to me differently, trying to get his voice to sound twenty years younger than his eyes. Mom had started making preparations. It was strange to see her so vibrant, so much younger than him. She'd just told me the news. We're going to have to leave, Demetrio, okay? Where. Buenos Aires, Demetrio, we're moving there. When. Soon, soon. I felt my stomach burn, my head dissolve. Then I didn't feel or say anything. Ever again. I ran along the shore, explored the little paths among the cedars, sat on the same boulders as I always had, peered into the hideouts built with cut limbs for when storms come. But I couldn't find her. Then I learned the truth: she'd been forbidden from going out and from seeing me. Then everything seemed so logical, so simple: one misfortune leads to another. I closed my eyes. I imagined the myrtles, the island shelters, and strained to carve them into the blank space behind my eyes, because I knew. It was so simple. It must be like being dead, I thought, and went back to the cabin and nothing had been moved, but everything had changed. I locked myself up in the room that was no longer mine and searched, like an idiot, for the tears I didn't have.

(Complete, defined, the roof receives a lash of light. The daisies rule the edges of the path. There is pollen, invisible, and hidden birds. There are fish that have known the water's end, the depths of a vast hand that cups itself in offering to the earth. There's heat and mountain slopes and pine groves farther out, then blue. Beyond it is a table and another hand, larger and smaller, with fingertips that brush against the landscape. There's a white wall, a feeble light bulb like the noose of someone illuminated. There's a chair, a man who never sleeps, a silent room. And there, at last, aflutter, is the scarlet specter of a haunting figure in a nightgown, her tempered pinecone breasts, an apparition floating past the windowpane, who contemplates, with eyes transparent as a baffled fish, the back and shoulders of the man, who hunches there in solitary labor at the living room table.)

XLVI

Verónica's heels echo for no one. Her skirt stops just above her knees. She smokes as she walks, and the gray drift blurs her hair. Her swaying handbag caresses her waist. Eight thirty. Her sons have just waved to her from the entrance of the school with such jubilation that it somehow makes her feel guiltier.

In Chacarita, the hubbub submerges. The mouth of the Lacroze subway stop methodically expels suits, backpacks, tatters, more suits, grime, briefcases. The candied-nut vendors release their crispy proclamations. Verónica cuts through the swarm, skirts the cemetery, and turns right.

She knows he's not yet home. She presses a buzzer at random. Who is it? Could you let me in, I forgot my key. Bug off. She presses another. Hi I'm canvassing for—Not interested, thanks. And another. Hello it's the mailman, ma'am! Ah the mailwoman? That's right ma'am yes! Alright, go ahead . . . Verónica pushes the door and squints for a clearer view of the hall. Too impatient to wait for the elevator, she takes the stairs.

She pauses for breath on the final landing. Almost at Demetrio's door, she hears noises from the neighboring apartment. She retreats and hurries down a few stairs. Soon an expansive woman stalks out as if every step involved a decision. Verónica cranes her neck a bit: the woman waits for the elevator, opens the grate, struggles to slide it shut, and vanishes down the shaft. Verónica heads back up as she opens her purse and extracts a white envelope. She hesitates briefly at Demetrio's door. She flexes her knees and crouches down, instinctively protecting her cleavage, even though she's alone. She slips the envelope under the door and flees down the stairs, among the clicks of her heels that echo for no one.

XLVII

I remember I said to him I said look you're crazy, what the hell are you talking about, this is some bullshit you're saying, and him, nothing, I mean whatever, he listened, like his eyes were moving around all over the place and he looked at my hands, I was fidgeting a lot cause he was saying all this stupid shit. You don't just go out and get another job, do you think it's easy to just get a job these days? No he said, no it's not that. Oh no? so what the hell is it then, huh, tell me. The thing is Negro if I had some other job it would just end up being the same, you know, or I don't know, pretty much the same. Okay listen Demetrio, lemme make sure I'm following you, are you fuckin sick of this or aren't you? Yeah Negro yes I am. Alright so what happens if you quit and then you don't find anything else cause, I don't know, cause who knows. Yeah, but I'm trying to tell you that that's not the issue here Negro, I don't think you get it, it's true I can't take it anymore but that's the consequence, right? No sir I don't get it okay, you're just trying to make things harder for yourself. God you're dense Negro. Maybe so but hey I have some peace of mind. At least making things harder means I've got more freedom. Oh yeah? and tell me what's the point of freedom if you're this fucked up in the head.

So we started hanging out less. Some mornings we fought, I didn't want to because you can't even argue with the guy, you know what I mean, he always has to have the last word cause mister Demetrio thinks he's real smart, he was real into books as a kid, he's like Verónica that way, birds of a feather, see what I'm saying. Also when I'm pissed off I can't think right, I start talking bullshit, I can't put two words together without swearing like a fuckin sailor and I get everything all mixed up, I got a temper on me what can I say, I don't try to act all posh like some people who always keep a cool head or whatever, what can I say, I didn't feel like fighting with Demetrio, I mean it. But then you know he looked so fuckin sure that how the hell was I not gonna ask him, he was my friend at the end of the day, you know what I'm saying, I mean what the hell man you got some money saved up somewhere or something? what the fuck are you gonna do without any money, man! I swear to god I thought he'd lost it, but anyways, what really did do a number on him was the thing with the hobo, that was a real bummer cause Demetrio thought, I don't know what he thought, he thought they were buddies or something, the idiot.

XLVIII

The revolving light swept an orange wake across the asphalt.
The grime of the day and the evening and its night were
fleetingly exposed, then darkened again. San Telmo was a
leathery skin, a scabbed surface awaiting relief. Tires plowed
the damp road. Bristling, a momentarily orange shadow
crossed at the corner of Bolívar and Venezuela.

They got out of the truck: Demetrio and the timid
shrimpy guy. El Negro was home with the flu and had sent
a substitute who studied Demetrio's every move with exas-
perating discipular attention. The shrimp asked fastidious
questions about the route, the pace, the schedule, always
in a tone of histrionic respect. Demetrio hated feeling like
anyone's teacher, much less a teacher of shit-collection. He
couldn't keep a sense of hostility from infusing his replies,
an aggression that at no point seemed to discourage the
substitute.

El Negro's uniform was like a gargantuan creature devour-
ing the shrimp's entire body except for his head, which peeked

out, nervous, and moved incessantly. Irked, Demetrio asked him why he hadn't brought his own uniform or requested a smaller one. The substitute stammered that he didn't have a uniform and there weren't any others, or there were, but they weren't his, or not entirely his, and every night he'd been picking out one that was more or less his size from among the available uniforms, but this time it so happened that the replacement uniforms were at the laundry, so he'd ended up using El Negro's, which worked just fine. Demetrio received the final bag on Calle Perú, awkwardly flung into the truck by the shrimp, who seemed to grapple more with himself than with the weight of the bags. They lied to you, moron, Demetrio yelled down, they never wash the uniforms, and I'm not so sure about that one you're wearing, maybe you'd do a better job in your birthday suit. The shrimp let out a stunned bark of laughter. Demetrio spotted a drain in the road and spat.

As they approached Calle 9 de Julio, Demetrio said nothing about the old Tacuarí beggar. He thought of him silently, imagining him curled up against the rusty iron door, sheltered in his coat, his hat a crease of shadow, resisting the oblique wind. He promised himself that he'd pay the guy a visit as soon as El Negro was better, hopefully tomorrow, he thought. The substitute had struggled to pull off his gloves and left them next to Demetrio's; now he was staring straight ahead with the vague look of a soldier awaiting orders. Demetrio gripped the wheel and stepped on the gas, not even turning his head when he drove past a certain bar on Calle Bolívar where the waiter, sleepy behind the counter, was arranging cups and feeling a little lonelier than usual. On their way to the dump, the shrimp suggested they stop for breakfast, we deserve it, right?, he ventured with a hopeful smile. I never eat breakfast, kid, Demetrio replied.

XLIX

My love,

I'm writing you this letter because we haven't seen each other in over a week and you haven't called either. I know it's not a great idea for me to pick up if El Negro is home, but it wouldn't be the end of the world, darling, remember how it happened once and you just pretended you needed to talk to him. It was dangerous and exciting. It made me a little horny actually. So what I think is that you just don't want to call me anymore, that you don't feel like talking like we used to. Remember when you said my voice was sweet as a flute? El Negro would never tell me things like that.

Demetrio, you know perfectly well that if we don't sleep together I can take care of myself, maybe I'd even find someone else, who do you think you are. I have a will and a mind of my own. But this is what I can't stand, when someone says they love me and I say me too, very much, and then two years go by, two years, Demetrio! And then you realize that all you got out of it were a few moments of feeling loved after orgasm. That's the way it is no matter what you say, I can almost hear you. Don't you get it, that it's the false hopes I can't stand? I'd rather have an asshole for a lover, someone who doesn't tell me anything and uses me and I know it and use him back. But you gave me false hopes, and I started believing you, little by little, and now I've been lying every day for two years while trying to be a good mom and a good housewife and a halfway decent wife too.

I don't care about the lying. I have a right to that and more, because the real sacrifice isn't having to work and bring home a paycheck every month or even killing yourself working two jobs like him. The real sacrifice is to stop working, to give that up. I could have chosen something else. That's your fault, you'd say. And it's true, you're right, Demetrio, it's my fault. But neither of you will ever understand what it means to carry around a life inside you, take care of it all by yourself, and learn to love it for almost a year while what you guys mostly do is just imagine it and stick your ear against my belly. I detached from my son and gave him to El Negro, I said here, here's the boy you wanted so bad, take him, I suffered for both of us. When the complications with my pregnancy started I had to stop working for four months, then a couple more months after I gave birth, and then when you want to go back to work the sons of bitches say they're so sorry but the company blah blah blah. They threw me a few cents and that was it. It would have taken ages to sue and cost us a fortune, as you know. And in the end El Negro had his son, who he was going to teach to kick the ball with both legs while he was still little so he'd get used to it, look how big he is, look how beautiful, we always said. You'll never know what it feels like after that, or why I thought almost without realizing it: of course, let him support his kid! Let him support us and repay me for that sacrifice. How could I have been so stupid? Now our oldest is in school and can't kick with his left, just like his dad.

So as you can see I couldn't care less about anything. But what I still can't stand is that I gave you things I never gave my husband, and now ten whole days go by and you wouldn't even know if I'd got hit by a train. I guess you probably thought of calling me whenever your dick felt like it, and then you'd ask me how are you, how are you feeling, you bloodsucker, you fucking overgrown child.

And that's why I'm writing to you, because I can't take ten days of this, Demetrio, I have to live too. Maybe I'm just a little corny, what can I say. Can't you see I'm not asking for much, I just want us to talk more often, love, and to listen to each other. I'll get old faster without your voice, I won't have the strength to hate my husband and know I deserve something better. You made me see that. So I'm asking you to please be true to those words that no one asked you for.

Waiting with love,

Verónica

L

The biggest suitcase, the black one with a single rusty handle, that one was mine and I carried it in silence. I also had a huge backpack that tugged me backward, I had to put my whole body into every step to keep from falling. My mom talked, gestured, organized everything, but her suitcase was small and had only clothes in it. And my old man, though the move had cheered him up some, had just two medium backpacks, and when we went to the station he dragged a kind of trunk full of woolen clothes that even mom could have lifted: now I was the strongest of the three. Which seemed impossible. I looked at my parents, who panted and sort of stared vacantly ahead, as if trying to make out something blurry in the distance, and then I felt full of energy and a confusion I'd never experienced before. I hurried up and clutched harder at the rough handle of the suitcase, more determined and more afraid.

We were waiting at the station, sitting on benches on the platform. We ate apples and didn't talk to each other. There weren't many people around. I remember, I don't know why, a kid who was playing with a little collectible toy car, the kind that looks like a mafia car or an old taxi, I remember because I used to have a Matchbox car just like it, with a high roof, and I thought it was funny because cars never looked like that except in movies. The kid played by himself and his mom wasn't paying attention. Suddenly the car zoomed away from him and landed on the rails, right there in the middle of the tracks. He looked all around as if waiting for someone to bring it back to him, he looked at me and I smiled but didn't react otherwise, the way adults do with kids, and he was getting more and more upset, and then I heard a loud noise, a kind of flute it sounded like at first, but then we saw the train and the noise got louder and closer. The kid sort of drifted indecisively toward the tracks, and I was about to call out to his mom, who was still deep in conversation with another woman, I was about to get up and go over, but in the end I didn't have to because the kid realized himself that he wasn't going to be able to save his car, and he settled for staring at it from the platform for the last time before whoosh!, the train passed and smashed it and the pieces didn't even fly out all over the place, just whoosh!, it disappeared and that was that. I think the kid kind of looked at me sidelong when he turned around, as if judging me for something, and then he went back to his mom.

The train was huge and old and had a yellow diesel engine, which disappointed me a little because I was expecting a locomotive with a smokestack and lots of smoke. The windows of the train cars were dirty and inside, strange, they had what looked like toy bunk beds, with ladders and everything. How long until we get there? I asked my mom, and my old man answered: about a day and a half, leave your mother in peace for a while won't you, she's exhausted, and it was true, she was sitting slumped on the bench, her eyes fixed on the ground, her hair disheveled, wearing a sweater that was too big for her. Thirty-six hours! so that was what the beds were for. Buenos Aires was farther away than I'd thought, though who could get any sleep on those wooden planks, Dad probably wouldn't even fit. We'd taken a coach bus to the station, but had Mom said it would be too expensive to take a bus the rest of the way, not that all our stuff would have fit, and in any case I liked the train better, my first train, because they'd said you could wander around the cars, and feel the vehicle rocking and swaying between them, and sometimes the train-wagons would brake abruptly to cool off, and then you could look out at the landscape and hear the silence.

The weather was cooling off. On the platform there was only a scrap of sun and no empty benches in sight. Some passengers started filing off the train and they looked around uncuriously at everything, their faces tired. Mom suddenly snapped to attention and said let's go, let's go, Dad signaled to me and I grabbed the huge suitcase again. My palms stung and it hurt to bend my fingers. We walked down the platform along the train, looking for our car, almost at the end, come on hurry up, my old man yelled to me, don't fall behind, but I was distracted by what I could see inside the windows, there were heads peering out, arms drooping like coat sleeves, and every so often I'd run a little to catch up with my parents, but then I'd slow down again. I was puzzled to see a guy reaching his compartment and hanging a damp towel in the window, and then I saw that there were other towels in other cars. As we boarded the train, my old man holding out an arm to my mom to help her up, I saw some yellow letters painted on the trembling steel: Estrella del Sur. Soon the train tooted its horn and then it didn't sound like a flute but some other, deeper instrument. What, what did you say? my old man barked, and I repeated my question louder, and then he answered: for the dust, kid, the towels are for the dust!

LI

The brilliant threads are interlaced, complete, across the crystal lake. The stony cliffs, their snowy peaks, lull the horizon. More than it ever has, the sky looks like a tile, the group of conifers a green mosaic out behind the cabin. Some blurry birds fly toward the sun; others retreat and hide inside the home the massive cedar offers them, the father of all trunks. And now, the finished path laps at the earth until it stops to drink from the Nahuel Huapi. It's flanked by sunbright daisies. There, a climbing cat regards the lake from up above, perched on the old slate roof. A halted flow that surges from the chimney, a fragile smoke sullies the day's precision.

LIII

Not in the hollow of the pedals, not on the seats, not tucked beside the spare tire. Not in the cubbies at the garage: they were nowhere to be found. El Negro sighed, not especially put out, with the triumphant look of someone enduring a setback he had predicted. He scratched his mustache and fell compassionately quiet. Not Demetrio, though. Demetrio, pale, was upholding a different silence, with the supposed dispassion that carves itself into defeated faces.

El Negro had returned to work the morning before. His three-day flu had dug a furrow under his eyes and left a trace of helplessness in his voice. Demetrio had felt unexpectedly relieved to see him in the garage, punctual as always, instead of the shrimpy apprentice. The day's pickup had been efficient, soothingly mechanical, free of idiotic questions, punctuated by the occasional off-color remark, the occasional perfunctory laugh. Every street was systematically dispossessed of its waste; the cats seemed to recognize them and didn't meow distrustfully or arch their backs. As soon as they crossed the corner of Independencia and Tacuarí, Demetrio signaled to El Negro and they both got out, cheerfully, even. The old man was waiting for them, wide-eyed as a squirrel, hugging his knees, the brim of his tattered hat tilted upward. Demetrio held out a gloved hand in greeting and the old Tacuarí beggar accepted it meekly.

The three men had eaten breakfast together like an oddball family. Demetrio, not quite sure why, beheld his companions affectionately and felt an urge to protect them. As they left the bar, exhaling the wintry fog, Demetrio had made the same suggestion as before. But this time the old man had said yes. They got into the truck and headed for the dump. Once they reached the garage, El Negro changed his clothes at top speed and waved a thick, affable hand goodbye. Checking occasionally to make sure the guard wasn't watching, Demetrio wandered with the old man around the multicolored mountain and narrated the junk's journey into the depths. The old Tacuarí beggar listened and nodded, smiling toothlessly. Later, worn out from the walk, he sat down and leaned back against the tire of one of the trucks. Then Demetrio suggested he stay and rest in the garage, bundled up and hidden from view, until Demetrio and El Negro returned early the next morning and took him back to Tacuarí. The old man eagerly accepted. It was easy to find a good spot beside the emergency truck, behind the heap of used tires that had been amassing in a corner for years. The old man said goodbye to Demetrio, mumbling words of gratitude. Demetrio donned his street clothes, left his uniform in the truck beside El Negro's, and cast a final glance into the back of the garage, where he could imagine the old Tacuarí beggar observing him backlit through a tire, or maybe already asleep.

El Negro had watched Demetrio show up a few minutes later than usual. He waited, leaning against the truck, arms crossed, face fixed with a sneer that was half-bitter, half-satisfied. He'd limited himself to gesturing at the cab of the truck, opening the door with a flourish. Demetrio ran to the back of the garage, kicking away several old tires, then retraced, now looking neither astonished nor troubled. For the sake of protocol, he rummaged around the glove compartment and under the seats. He knew their uniforms wouldn't be in the cubbies, but he went to check anyway. Then, finally, he took his seat at the wheel while El Negro brought two suits that weren't theirs. Now Demetrio stared out into the void, into the putrid mass, barely visible in the dark.

LIIII

It was a real bummer, the thing with the hobo, I know it hurt him more than he said, he tried to play it cool but he couldn't fool me, gimme a break. I remember the look on his face, it was just a second but I'll never forget it, where did you put the uniforms Negro where did you leave them?, that's impossible, are you sure Negro?, man don't look at me like that, help me look . . . He wasn't wondering for long. Then he calmed down real quick and realized what happened, shit man, I mean he knew right from the beginning, he just didn't want to accept it, and whatever, I said to him, don't freak out Demetrio, what's done is done, come on get changed, use this smaller one, it'll fit you great, this one's a liiittle tight on me but it works, come on hurry up brother it's getting late.

And he was fine all morning, I remember we had a great breakfast, we were even both in a pretty good mood. The problem was when we got to Tacuarí, uh-oh, that's when I thought ah shit, now he's gonna want to go find the geezer, he's gonna go off on him, we fucked up. But no, not at all, actually he went and said Negro why don't you go and I'll stay put, it's just a few bags anyway right? Yeah bro of course I said, you got it, and I got out by myself and you know, tell you the truth, I have to admit I did sneak a look at that doorway cause the curiosity was killing me, I just had to see if he was there, what can I say. But no one was there, I mean whatever, I didn't look too hard but I don't think so, and when I got back into the truck Demetrio didn't ask either.

I thought he could use a vacation, you know it pissed me off a little I gotta say, I work twice as much as you and I'm not such a pain in the ass, I say to him, you live alone and don't need much to get by, I don't know, it's not right, a guy breaks his back working and then it turns out it's the wimp who's had it up to here. But anyways, it seemed to me like mostly he just needed a break and that was it, I don't know, take a trip to the countryside or something, I mean he's from the countryside anyways isn't he?, a few days chilling out and good to go, he'd stop taking everything so goddamn serious. But yeah I mean considering what happened, now I guess probably he should've gotten the hell out of there earlier, out of all that shit instead of staying put until he really couldn't take it anymore.

LIV

He saw her writhe as if searching for something with her arms. He couldn't see himself, but Demetrio was able to take himself in aerially, to imagine his own body from the back, atop another body. From this specular vision, he tried to melt into her, but he could barely acquiesce with some rhythmic contractions. He sought out some suggestive detail, maybe her touch on his neck, or those soft breasts that jostled and dispersed, but it all seemed useless: none of it was happening to him. And why moan, he shouted silently at Verónica, sex happens all by itself, without us. There were, however, a few moments when Demetrio relented, when he came to believe that he was mistaken, hearing vaguely oh yes yes harder don't stop just like that oh yes. Then he'd felt himself gradually fade out, things tended toward haziness, he was no longer so sure of what day it was, of where he was, what room number, and then he felt how another voice joined the chant and the mirror shattered and the keen slivers rained down on his back and punctured his flesh, a luscious harm.

A bolt of lightning cracked across his timeline, declaring the end, the blindness snatched away his strength, and he fell. Then they kissed, sweetly, and he loved her more than ever or like always or like he did before. But all it took was an excess embrace for the mirror to reassemble itself and fly back into the ceiling of the room, for the body clutching his to become a strange presence once more.

Lying on his back now, he closed his eyes and imagined a shore. It was night and everything waited. The water swept a murmur in its current and delicately broke, he could hear crickets and some bird or other, the air was cool and slipped against his skin. He took a deep breath, noting how the night seeped into his lungs and filled them with tiny stars. Then he reached out, groping, found other fingers lacing his own. He felt a serene thigh and knew at once that there, a little farther up, would be a fine white nightgown, a belly like a shrine, a distant face, and at the pinnacle, some incendiary threads. He felt those fingers summoning him to resurrection and to a second death, and, inflamed by their touch, he threw himself onto her once and for all.

LV

(The end of day, the shattering. The peaks incite a troubled sky. The rock breaks loose, scratching the back of the colossus. Staring into the waters of the Perito Moreno, the face of Cerro López startles at the sight of its decrepitude. The wind roams aimlessly among the summits, through erratic snow, toward clouds rehearsing violet deaths.)

Our new place was on a narrow cobblestone street. More bicycles passed than cars, kids played and shouted, a sweet chaos up and down the block. We lived on the third floor, not too high but a bizarre novelty for me, the experience of walking and sleeping on top of your neighbors. The kitchen was dark, my old man always complained about that, there's no light in here dear, don't you think we should put a window in, I mean it shouldn't be so dark, and my mom always answered that, considering everything we still hadn't bought, how could we possibly spend money on a hole so she could peel onions in the sunlight, come on don't be silly, enough dreaming. There was a little washing area for clothes in the back. Then we'd hang up our laundry on ropes under the dining room window, and since we shared it with the neighbors we had to take turns. Frankly, I don't know, it was hard for us, being surrounded by all those people. Where we came from, on the outskirts of Bariloche, a neighbor meant a guy who had a house ten minutes from yours, so every once in a while you'd go and ask him for some wood, or in the summer we'd run into him swimming in the Nahuel Huapi or in the Moreno. But in Lanús the buildings were narrow and squat and the doors were all on top of each other, it was like living in a beehive, and even so my old man said it was even worse in the capital and more expensive also. My room was a small square with two beds in case my brother Martín came back. It was almost empty, there was just a closet with a pile of wallpapered boards and a metal tube for hangers. I put all my things there except for two books and my jigsaw puzzles, which I'd leave on the floor or in an old fruit box Dad had sanded and painted for me, here, turn it upside down and you've got a bedside table. In those days I never kept the puzzles intact after putting them together, it didn't make sense to me, now though, I need something that isn't broken. The two books were yellow and hardbound and on the cover they had a drawing of some historical figures and a list of other book titles on the back. I didn't like that the characters were drawings, I wanted to imagine they had different faces every time. The type was very small and the thick pages were worn-out. I loved to smell them. The best thing about the house was the water, which you didn't have to heat in pots because we had a huge boiler in the kitchen, you just had to be patient and it would come out great. Mom and Dad had to sleep sort of crammed together but they never complained about that. Every morning my old man and I went out to look for work, him with the newspaper under his arm, coughing, and my mom would get mad and say he hadn't been keeping warm enough.

(The mountain's gaze is vertical. The shadows, indecisive. There's something swarming in the lake that churns the sketches on the water, something vigorous and deep. The outlines shift without establishing themselves, then reappear and vanish out of sight. There are no birds, no drizzling rain, the sky is clear for now, just reddened—bruised—by a few clouds in silent detonation.)

LVI

When Demetrio burst into the darkness like a feeble coal, and in a uniform that wasn't his, it was exactly four o'clock in the morning. With the hostile breath of the Río de la Plata stiffening his lips, he let a compact almond of spit slip through his mouth and onto a sewer grate, watching the foamy matter spread across a couple of the bars until it fell in. Pleased, he wiped his lips dry. El Negro spoke to him. He didn't respond, engrossed in the bars, suspended. El Negro grew impatient, invoked the company's possible reprisals. Demetrio's deafness seemed to deepen. He stood stiff-shouldered, as if he'd forgotten to drop them. The voice of the void ran down Independencia until it reached 9 de Julio, not stopping at the other narrow streets they'd visit. El Negro's gloved paw struck Demetrio on the shoulder, not violently per se, although it did convey the warning of less friendly swipes in the future. A sigh cracked Demetrio's paralysis. He adjusted his gloves and crouched to grasp two bags by the knots and toss them up to El Negro with total precision, then immediately dropped down again and flung more bags into the outstretched arms of his partner, who gradually deposited them into the hull of the truck as Demetrio sent another pair arcing upward.

The morning had progressed with great effort, as if the hours were limping. Calle Defensa received them apathetic and catless. Calle Bolívar proved predictable with every culling of waste. Calle Perú offered them its grime with a kind of trim hospitality. On the corner of Chacabuco and Humberto Primo, someone had discarded a standing lamp that Demetrio thought, for an instant, due to some kind of optical illusion, was inexplicably on. Along Piedras, between Chile and México, they found that all the bags were punctured. Dogs, cats, and unforeseen circumstances had apparently joined forces to expose the neighborhood's intestines, spilling its secrets. Demetrio dawdled over some diapers that stood out amid the putrefaction, foreign in their whiteness against the black plastic, blindingly youthful in the sweep of expiration: those delicate diapers that, indeed, barely concealed their true contents. On the final stretches of Calle Tacuarí, Demetrio opted to stay inside the truck.

Turning onto Avenida San Juan, El Negro finally glimpsed the first frozen student, a girl, walking quickly, but this time he found no complicity in Demetrio, no smile. Their usual parking spot was occupied by a van, so they were forced to take a detour along Paseo Colón, where there were far more taxis and the bus windows fogged with yawning mouths. At that hour, the city started to expel them somehow. They, who worked so hard to beautify it. Like neon intruders, they'd lifted the final bags with a vague sense of inhibition they never expressed in words.

They had café con leche and not entirely warm toast for breakfast at the bar on Bolívar. They spoke intermittently and little. The waiter asked how it was going and El Negro said not too bad, working. Just like everybody else, my man, just like everybody else. Not easy. But we gotta keep fighting the good fight, you know? That's right, what else can you do. That's right. Demetrio saw a tiny jellyfish of milk-skin floating in his coffee. He grimaced, repulsed, and said nothing. There were two other customers in the bar. One was so fat he overflowed his own edges. The other, dressed in all black, sat with his eyes closed, looking like a passed-out priest.

LVII

(. . . it looks like a calandra lark, maybe a woodlark. Perhaps a fraying thread of smoke adrift . . . The cloud is incomplete, the sky won't fuse together, it's chopped up . . . A bird cutting across. Or no, a shadow . . . And the reflection on the lake? Pieces are missing. Any more of the dark ones? Maybe farther back . . . He watches clouds rehearsing their own violet death, splitting in silence, and nonetheless . . . There's nothing to be done about it, no solution.)

He'd get up around two in the morning, my old man. He'd get home at noon, eat something, read the paper, spend a little time with us, and go to bed early, because he had to start making bread at 3 A.M. sharp. I think that's when I developed my taste for keeping weird hours. He said I should stay home and help my mom, who was all alone. That he could support us and if he couldn't we'd figure something out later. That the house needed fixing up and that's what I was there for, now that I was a man and all. My mom kept saying the cold was to blame. She was always rehashing the same stuff, poor thing, as if it would comfort her to know the exact reason. It's because he's always going out so early, and in the winter, she'd insist. But I know perfectly well that we'd heard Dad coughing for a long time.

(The cliff that plunges to the other side . . . Some scrap of day, above, far off . . . Where are the missing smudges on the lake?)

What I don't get is how the hell I stayed home like an idiot, painting a door green or peeling vegetables with Mom. What the hell was I waiting for, instead of going out and telling him no, just one second sir, you stay here, I'm the one who's going to work, I'm stronger, you rest. Or at least take over half his morning shift, I don't know, something. Instead, I filled my room with furtive cigarettes and puzzles.

(And do they rupture silently, those clouds?)

We managed to put up some curtains in the dining room and Dad brought in a secondhand couch, mustard-yellow, that could be converted into a double bed. It was pretty ugly, it had these tall rectangular cushions. I added the wooden leg it was missing.

(Below, the current doesn't freely run, the water falters into empty space . . . As for the pine grove that's supposed to be beside the lake, it's now impossible.)

A used couch, but it was comfortable, I mean, whatever, it was fine. It didn't creak when you got up. I tightened the springs.

(The night half-falls, doesn't improve . . .)

He was lying right there, on that couch, when the pneumonia started.

(He's tried them all, and no piece fits among the peaks, or manages to sink beneath the surface of the lake, or wants to travel to the clouds or snow.)

LVIII

The water karate-thwacked his shoulders. He flashed vaguely on a beating he'd been dealt in a dream. The steam licked the bathroom tiles. Demetrio scoured his whole body with soap, crowned himself with shampoo, and let the water jostle his brain. He watched the suds course between his ankles, trailing milky signs: he imagined his gray hairs, the ones he'd have or was starting to have, roving the drains of the building.

He looked for a clean towel. There was only one left. He scrubbed himself as if he were made of someone else's matter. His skin was drier, or maybe his towel had gotten coarser, scattered with little barbs of thread. When he reached his thighs, he stopped to study his penis, pink and heat-softened. It looked like a ridiculous fruit. He cradled his testicles in one hand and let the gland bloom in the other. The towel dropped to the floor. Demetrio decided to masturbate and sat down on the edge of the tub, drawing the towel closer with his feet. Right away, he thought he heard a distant whistle, ignored it, his pulse quickened, he closed his eyes and kept going, only to recognize the ring of the phone in the living room, now loud and clear. He stopped. He didn't go to pick it up. The whistle soon went silent. He looked at himself clutching his balls, dazed, waiting for the phone to ring again.

Uh, hello? Hi, it's me. Hi. Why didn't you pick up? I was sleeping. Wait, still? do you know what time it is? Yes I know Verónica, tell me what you want. I want to talk to you, Jesus, what else would I want. Okay great, here I am, go ahead. What do you mean go ahead! don't you remember it's Sunday and Boca's the home team? Oh yeah, El Negro told me on Friday we were playing, maybe I'll join him, I haven't gone in forever . . . hello? Are you there, Vero? Yes I'm here you bastard, you're a fucking bastard and I hate you, you hear me! Yes of course, how would I not hear you if you're screaming in my ear. Do you think you can just mistreat me and I'm going to let you get away with it? Hey Vero look, so you wake me up to insult me, would you please calm down a little okay. You're so wrong if that's what you think, so wrong! You've been making so many demands that my balls are dragging on the floor by now, I don't think I'm wrong about that. You listen to me Demetrio, maybe you're scared to call me at home so I always have to be the one to call you, maybe I have to settle for almost nothing almost never, and maybe I even have to nag for us to see each other and you almost never take the initiative, but you know what?, this isn't working anymore, I'm done putting up with this. Look Vero, I don't think it's true that we don't see each other much, maybe lately yeah, but when we saw each other more often you complained anyway, the problem here is that you always want more, sometimes it seems like except for your kids you spend all day thinking about cheating on your husband. That's a new low for you, Demetrio Rota, unbelievable! Don't be mad love I'm sorry, okay you're right, listen here's what we'll do, I'll get dressed and eat something real quick and head over there, alright? No, not alright, I've had enough, this isn't happening anymore, you got it?, not like this. Okay Vero then like how, hm? Oh it's very simple honey, what I want is to leave my husband for good and pack my bags and move in together, that's it. Oh for chrissake that again!, and what about the kids, huh? We already talked about this Demetrio, at first they'll stay with their grandma, that's what she's there for, you know she's dying to control them and she's always crossing me, so good, all set, let her move in with her son and take care of my boys for a while, we can take turns till the dust settles, and then you've got a spare room at your place for the kids right?, I mean I already have some money saved up anyways, or you know what's even better actually!, it would be even better if I came over right away with the kids, and on weekends they can stay with their dad and grandma, they should always spend weekdays with me so I can take them to school which they're used to anyway, it wouldn't be much work for you,

I'll deal with them, come on Demetrio, I love you, can't you see I can't keep living in this house knowing you're there all alone in yours? Demetrio . . . ? Uh I don't know, Verónica look, I'm not so sure, you'll burn through your savings really fast, and the kids need . . . Their father would support the kids just like he's doing now for fuck's sake, that has nothing to do with us! besides I know perfectly well what they need, don't worry about me I'll figure it out, and speaking of, you could look for another job don't you think. Don't you dare tell me what to do, watch yourself. Sweetie all I'm trying to say is this doesn't have to be so hard for us, just think about it! Yes Vero I've thought about it lots of times and what I'm saying is we can't live together, you know that. But why, tell me why! Because we can't, because I can't. Very good! okay very good perfect, whatever you say, but you listen to me: if you don't want to be together after all this time, if you don't have the balls to take the next step, then I'm leaving you. Oh yeah is that what you're doing? Yessir, you can be sure of that. Ah, got it . . . What do you mean ah, what do you mean ah, I'm being serious here. Are you saying you'd rather end it all than meet up some days like we are now? Well look who's paying attention. So basically it's all black and white to you? The thing is you're never going to understand me, oh God, you're leaving me so alone. Be alone if that's what you want Vero, why don't we calm down and you can sleep on it. Because I've thought too much already, and if I can't live the way I want then I'd rather not think there's another life out there, chau Demetrio, see you never, at the end of the day you're the one who's really alone because you don't know how to love anyone at all.

LIX

In the middle of the plaza, the campfire shone like an orange bush battered by wind. The old Tacuarí beggar looked at it for the last time and then turned away, limping. He was bleeding above one eye and his ribs hurt. He hesitated for a moment. He thought of turning back, but the hostile stares from the other vagrants dissuaded him.

Avenida 9 de Julio looked so vast and desolate that the changing colors of the traffic lights seemed like a taunt, an error of the night. In the distance, the obelisk emphasized the scrawling of a blurry sky. The old Tacuarí beggar tugged up the collar of his coat and hobbled forth. He could still hear the others in the plaza, insulting him, celebrating his flight with drunken cascades of laughter. Pressing on, he lowered his head and looked down at his dirty bare feet. He could understand why they'd stolen his food and the bench where he slept, he could even understand why they'd beat him up for refusing to leave the plaza—but why would they want a pair of old boots they weren't even going to wear? As he struggled to his feet, they hadn't even let him retrieve the boots when one of the men flung them into the road.

Now the old Tacuarí beggar limped down Independencia on frozen feet and ankles. Ringed by tattered silhouettes, the fire shrank in the distance: a bird of light that flapped and fluttered without ever taking wing.

LX

Not far from his apartment, in a small shop in the western part of Lanús, Demetrio was hired as watchmaker's apprentice. Working from ten to two and four to eight for fat Mascardi, he had initially been confined to organizing spare coils, rods, wheels, springs, and winders by size, to punching minuscule perforations in leather straps for wristwatches, and, most of all, to washing the windows and sweeping the floor at the end of the day.

As Demetrio slowly gained his trust, fat Mascardi began allowing him to examine the quartz in electronic clocks, or, if there wasn't too much work, he'd explain the extraordinary mechanics of the last revolution: atomic cesium clocks. Time changes with the times, kid! the fat man would exclaim, delighted. And as far as Demetrio was concerned, he was right: he himself had had to break with his age and grow up fast, just as his mother had predicted. Those predictions, however, hadn't accounted for the fact that there would be only two of them at home.

With his first paycheck from the clock and watch shop, Demetrio had bought his mother a used TV set with a respectable picture quality, if you applied two clothespins to the tips of the antennae and a third clothespin to the channel dial. She was getting back to normal in those days: she entertained herself by watching soap operas, slept some at night, went shopping on her own. When Demetrio came home from work, they'd eat dinner together while watching the news, then talk about clocks or Martín; never about his father. Some months back, at his medical check-up for military service, Demetrio had been exempted for his abnormally flat feet. In any case, now that he'd have to be the breadwinner, he wouldn't have been forced to serve like his brother, who sent word of his plans to become a career soldier and added that certain problems in the Neuquén barracks prevented him, for the time being, from visiting them in Buenos Aires. Demetrio smoked more than ever. He kept up with his puzzles on weekends. Above his bed, he'd taped up a photo of Marilyn Monroe, whose unfaltering smile supervised his solitary sex life. He hadn't written any letters in a while. In any case, she'd never written back.

He was fat Mascardi's apprentice for almost a year. With the old savings gone and his salary plateaued, Demetrio started frequenting the capital until, one day around noon, he returned home with a new job as an assistant in a clock and watch shop on Calle Esmeralda. The commute was long: a train to Constitución, a bus downtown, then several blocks on foot. But there they'd pay him almost twice what he earned in Lanús. Demetrio, in spite of everything, was fond of fat Mascardi and occasionally stopped by to visit. The fat man would greet him, rattling like a maraca, the pockets of his blue apron stuffed with tiny gears and screwdrivers, and invite him to share some yerba mate. Time changes with the times, kid! Although, by then, Demetrio had begun to suspect that time didn't change at all for some people in this life.

LXI

Freedom?, man what can I say, it always seemed like something you probably shouldn't look for if you can't afford it. Demetrio was always busting my balls about that, that you had to be free, as if, you know, as if you could just like bam! to hell with it all. Sorry buddy I always said to him, I'd rather think about feeding my kids, but he stopped listening and we really couldn't talk anymore anyways. That's how bad it got.

Something crazy, that's what he must have done. The waiter at the bar had already said something to me about it, and when I realized he just took off like that, you know just chau!, and then he didn't show up one day and then another day and another, and I called him and he didn't answer, then I went and looked for him at home. I was out there ringing the buzzer for a long time and I left all worried, and that night I called him again but nope nothing. We didn't hear anything for days until finally I got through to the landlord and the guy told me that Demetrio had told him he was leaving, that he'd let him know out of the blue, like five six days ago, that he paid the month's rent and straight up moved out. I knew something was up, I know the kid like the back of my hand and you could tell something was up with him, god knows what. But you never imagine this sort of thing, like we were friends for a reason and he could've at least said something before he goes and disappears like that, you know what I'm saying? Hey Negro look I'm quitting, or I'm moving back south, whatever. But no, he just hauled off and disappeared, it's crazy.

One thing though is that he didn't take everything, he left dishes, some clothes, blankets, decorations, cigarettes!, and I don't think he even smoked actually, stop with the cigarettes Negro you can't get it up if you smoke, the bastard always said, joking you know. He left lots of stuff at his place, as if he'd just went away on vacation, but yeah no, cause then why would he tell the guy he was leaving, or why didn't he say anything at work and ask for some time off, unpaid leave's not hard to get. Actually you know something, we're not even really sure what he took with him, he wasn't the kind of guy who bought lots of shit and he didn't spend money on clothes or anything, he was always wearing the same shoes and two or three pairs of pants I always saw on him and those were still in the closet, or maybe he had more, what do I know. Or maybe the place always looked like that, half-empty. And fuck man, at the end of the day it hurts that your buddy skips town without saying nothing, as if there wasn't any trust there, you know. I'm not judging him, right, I mean to each crazy fucker his own, but the thing is we cared about him at home, you get me, I don't know what he did or if something happened to him, nobody but god knows that, but look we really cared about the guy, like when my wife found out Demetrio was gone she was crying the whole day, poor thing.

LXII

He waited expectantly for the light to change, as if it were a matter of luck. He had a hastily wrapped rectangular package under one arm. The opposite sidewalk was fragmented by noise and speed. The morning light broke over the rooftops and fell shattered onto the street's dirty mosaic. A dog took pains to shit precisely between the first two stripes of the crosswalk.

Demetrio was exhausted, an exhaustion that seared his eyelids and sheathed his entire head like a helmet. The pain in his temples thrummed to the beat of his blood. He raised his eyes beyond the traffic light. He could make out several workers perched in a labyrinth of scaffolding, executing arachnid movements amid the iron bars; behind them stood an old facade with caryatids and balconies. All that was left of its grand picture windows were some holes revealing a wrecked interior, shreds of plaster hanging from walls that were still absurdly, exquisitely wallpapered. The decapitated caryatids sustained a weight that had been lost. Dense green mesh was draped over where the main entrance should have been. Patches of moss grew, disoriented, on some of the windowsills. Demetrio saw one of the workers stretch dangerously, risking a fall. His fellows wove their way toward where he was supporting himself with one arm, not fully confident in the rope that bound his waist to the facade.

The tiny pedestrian on the traffic light began to blink, and when Demetrio turned to look at him, he had already gone green and silent as a chameleon. People crossed back and forth. Demetrio hesitated, wondering whether he should set out or keep watching the men in the scaffolds. Suddenly he felt as if the entire street were watching him, paralyzed at the green light, but he glanced back at the fresh moss on a caryatid, right there, a faint moss coating its armpits, and the stoplight started pulsing swiftly, the drivers clutched their wheels, the entire corner vibrated in preparation for a roar, and then Demetrio abruptly lurched into the crosswalk. As soon as he reached the other side, he heard the engines pass, licking at his back.

A foosball table hung vertically in the window display. The players floated in midair. There were dolls arranged on one side of it, balls on the other. Also laser guns, a Rambo-style survival kit, and an assortment of light sabers. Above them, Christmas wreaths and garlands amalgamated their glimmers with the flashes on the street. Below, among blonde dolls and reflected balconies, were trolls and elves, looking like monstrously tiny children.

Demetrio threaded his way around boxes, bicycles, and more boxes. He approached the counter and set down the package he was carrying. An android-eyed clerk interrogated him with her gaze and he gestured to the counter. She looked at the package quietly. Demetrio opened it, impatient, and exposed a five-hundred-piece puzzle box. It depicted the sun sinking into the mountains on the shores of an enormous lake. The clerk stared intently at the landscape on the box, at the unsettling permanence of the water's ebb and flow. He rapped the photo with the palm of his hand, and he said: Here, there you go, it doesn't work. What do you mean it doesn't work? the puzzle, you're saying? Yes yes, it's badly made. That would be very strange, sir. I'm telling you this puzzle is defective. How can you be sure? Because I can't do it, it won't come together, it's the first time this has happened to me in twenty years!

The clerk seemed to wake up or receive an electric shock. She looked at him, frightened, and backed away, slipping along as if on wheels, in search of an older woman who, following a tense exchange with the clerk, offered to give Demetrio a refund. In a mellifluous voice, she also offered to exchange the puzzle for a different one. But Demetrio said no, he didn't want that, and collected the money and left without wishing her a nice day.

LXIII

Martín had written to say he was coming to visit the next week. The same day his mother and brother received the letter, stamped from Neuquén, Martín called them from the Constitución station saying he was about to take a taxi to the house.

Demetrio hadn't seen his brother for a long time. Martín hadn't been home since the first summer of military service or even after that, when he'd heard the news of his father's death. At the funeral, their mother had wept for two different absences, two opposing voids. Demetrio, though, wasn't really surprised by his brother's decision. Skipping the service was just like getting himself expelled from school, picking out clothes that would scandalize his family, spending his allowance on a motorcycle, or disappearing with his friends during a trip: it was all about snubbing a father who'd named him without his consent, compulsory heir to his authority. Demetrio had grown up both worshipping that powerful figure and burdened by the responsibility of assuming his duties. In family conflicts, he hadn't always resisted the temptation of taking his father's side. His older brother had reacted by accusing Demetrio of betrayal: because of his excessive submission, the family had turned out the way their father had made sure it would, just with one less person in it.

Demetrio and his mother fought at breakfast that morning. Martín's letter rested, equidistant, in the center of the table. At first, she announced that she would refuse to welcome her ungrateful son. But it didn't take long for Demetrio to convince her that this was an opportunity to talk and make amends. Maybe he wants to apologize too, he said, not masking how badly he longed to reconcile with Martín or noting the significance of his *too*.

Home from work, Demetrio found that his mother had not only changed her mind, but had also made a tarta de queso, one of Martín's favorite foods. Demetrio elected not to remind her that it was actually he, Demetrio, not his brother, who used to ask for the tarta as a child. I'm so nervous, dear, his mother said, hugging him in the kitchen, cloudy-eyed.

At five minutes to nine that night, Martín cleared the doorway with a resolute stride. He stopped in front of his mother, let himself be repeatedly kissed, and advanced toward Demetrio, who waited, not sure whether he should hold out a hand for a prudent shake or run and throw his arms around him. His brother's face had changed. Or, better put, the look of him had changed, his overall expression; his face, except for his two-day beard, was exactly as Demetrio remembered it. His brother crushed his broad chest into his own, slapping him vigorously on the back. When Demetrio tried to do the same, Martín had already pulled away and squared himself at the entrance to the living room, as if awaiting orders to sit. His mother tried to take his backpack, but Martín pushed her arm away with moderate zeal and dumped his luggage onto the couch. In his uniform and army boots, Martín looked tall, much taller than his father.

They ate amid discreet questions and eloquent silences. Martín answered with unwavering consideration and detachment, as if presenting an official report on his activities. He was satisfied with his position at the barracks. At the end of his service, he'd been named corporal of his squad and would soon be promoted to first corporal. Military routines were good for his health. Demetrio sensed how his mother tried, cautiously and without success, to steer the conversation toward the past, toward Bariloche. But all her diplomacy collapsed, along with all of Demetrio's suppositions, as soon as Martín, tasting the still-hot tarta de queso with something less than enthusiasm, suddenly asked: So how'd the old man die anyway?

The brothers sat in the kitchen to talk before bed. There was a bottle of red wine and a soda siphon on the table. Demetrio learned that Martín had met a girl from Río Negro and they'd been together for over a year. So that's why you never

came huh?, he said, trying to transmit a sense of complicity.
No Demetrio, his brother replied, she's the one who convinced me to come. Demetrio poured himself another glass
of wine; Martín had barely touched his. If it weren't for her,
I never would've thought so much about this, and by the
look of Mom, I think I did the right thing in coming now.
It would have been the right thing anytime Martín, don't be
stupid. Hold on Dem, you have no idea how hard it was for
me to make up my mind, maybe it doesn't make any sense
to you because you never left, you were always so sheltered
here, but now . . . But now what Martín, but now what,
everything would've been easier if you'd come back a long
time ago, don't you get it. And don't you get that it's not the
same now as it was before because Mom's much older than a
few years ago? Demetrio didn't answer; they sat quietly for a
while. Look Demetrio, you and me could've changed a ton
of things in this family, but you decided which one of us
would have to lose out, me or Dad, and you chose Dad and
now it's your turn, so take good care of Mom and pay her
back for everything she sacrificed, I have no debts and that's
why I'm doing great, that's always how it works, someday
you'll understand.

LXIV

He wore a black wool sweater and a gray scarf around his unshaved neck. His faded jeans adapted tenuously to his legs and groin. He was wearing boots with thin rubber soles that no longer smelled of leather, disfigured by patience. Demetrio got a feel for the street as he walked. He'd dressed carefully that evening.

He carried a khaki-colored backpack of a kind that no store had sold for years. He wore it slung across one shoulder and listed slightly to the side as he walked. The backpack thumped against one of his jean pockets and a few coins clinked inside. Keys, he thought out of habit, alarmed. Then he felt his other pocket and remembered he didn't need them now. He clicked his tongue. His mouth tasted like coffee and it bothered him; he was thirsty.

He stopped and waited for the light to change on Avenida San Juan. As the cars passed, he slipped both his arms through the backpack straps and tightened them. The pack contained several boxes of finished jigsaw puzzles, painstakingly glued onto cardboard bases: the alpine inn, the cabin on the lake, the lake beside an enormous pine grove, the purple sky over the mountain peaks, the little boats approaching a forest of myrtles. He was also carrying some warmer layers and a wallet. The cars stopped. A police siren or fire truck or ambulance shrilled in the distance. Demetrio crossed the street. He turned onto Bolívar, where he saw fewer people than cats. He glanced at his watch and crossed to the bar.

The waiter, incredibly, was the same guy as in the morning, the dim lighting was the same, the smell of ammonia, the emptiness of the space was all the same. Demetrio propped his elbows on the counter, ordered café con leche, and then immediately said no, actually make it a double whiskey. I'm surprised to see you so late, sir. Yeah. What brings you to this part of town? Just out for a walk. And the backpack? Demetrio intercepted the glass before it touched the counter. My backpack? Are you taking a trip? Yeah, a trip. Hey lucky you, glad to hear it. Yeah. It was cheap whiskey. Demetrio drank it quickly and stood up. What do I owe you. Hm, let's see, for you?, same as a coffee and toast. The waiter winked and straightened the stained collar of his shirt. Thanks for that, and you know what?, I actually came to say goodbye. Very kind of you sir, you have a good day and a good trip, it's going to be strange to see your friend having breakfast here without you. Demetrio didn't answer as he opened the door and confronted the cold.

He got off the bus. He walked up a paved slope for a while. There won't be many stars, he thought, looking up. After a final stretch of dirt road, panting a bit, he reached the dump. There was no detectable activity around it. He adjusted his scarf. He turned onto a cement path until he saw the garage and the great mass. He quickened his step. From that angle of the city outskirts, on the pedestal of waste, the sun was altogether out of sight. The temperature was dropping. The air seemed to convey flecks of frozen stench. He came to a stop a few meters from the mouth of the garage. Scattered notes of a Manzi tango, always tango, fluttered out to him: the motionless guard, who liked to recline his seat back against the wall of his cubicle and listen to the radio, looked like he was longing for too many things at once. Demetrio figured the old guy wouldn't ask questions if he just casually walked by, but he decided to take the long way around, just in case.

The perimeter was longer than he'd calculated. For a moment he had the feeling that he'd gotten the wrong place, the wrong strategy, the wrong night; that this couldn't possibly be the same garage as always, the same dirty and familiar place. Just as the wall was starting to feel truly interminable, its length petered out. Demetrio turned left, then left again. By contrast, the parallel wall looked far too short. Was the garage shaped like a trapezoid? He couldn't say, though he'd known it from the inside for years now. He glanced behind him, felt colder. He cinched the straps on his backpack. He walked the final stretch and heard, once again, a congested voice crooning about desolate nights and some old girlfriend's lover. He saw the paved path he'd taken before and retook it, advancing toward the fetid mass that seemed, too, bound for their encounter. In the fresh-fallen darkness, he thought he heard a murmur, a sound like water trickling over rocks. He listened harder and realized it was a machine raking through trash. Or maybe nothing, just the general rumble of the city down below, sprawled out like an indolent beast. That was when he noticed he couldn't hear the tango anymore; it felt like he'd been walking in a state of total unconsciousness. He looked back and picked out the tiny garage in the distance.

As he approached the end of the paved path, the puffs of air grew ranker. He'd never been so close to the edge of the dump before. Demetrio couldn't understand why the air was suddenly charged with sound, a truck out of sight, some crickets, a nearby crunch like bones or little pieces rattling in a box. He started intently ahead and saw the mass in all its details, the irregular slope, the lumpy surface like a mountain of bodies writhing or going still, and then it was more like the mass grave of all cities at night, what time was it?, he was struck by how, in the woozy glow of the bulbs and the moon blurred behind the clouds, the glimmers of buried glass were all green, what was really inside all those millions of bags?, which were his?, would he be able to retrieve them? The cement dropped off and he stepped on damp earth.

Under his feet, a few meters away, breathed all the excrescence of the world. His vision drifted out into a horizon of mysteriously organized fragments, countless heads peeking up from the ground and into the night, straining for oxygen. Demetrio struggled to understand, good god, how there could possibly be so much, this much shit. More than moving around like individual creatures, the waste seemed to tend toward fusion, it was all so uniform, plastic, filth, and silence, the convulsion came from below, from deep deep down, he could sense it in his frozen feet, it was a green, subterranean tremor that knit together a single skin, the skin of the One True Shit, the sea of the drowned. He stared very steadily into the epicenter of the monster: a sea or maybe a prehistoric lake, one with an impossible name, and the night slowly lit the surface of the Nahuel Huapi, it smelled of damp, of stone, the dark earth yielded and emanated, the sky and the water growled like rival bears, the cold stiffened their colors. He took two more steps and stopped right at the edge, inhaled a breeze composed of many tiny breezes; the night was about to happen, there was something like a muscle-tremor in the damp. He felt something slipping over his shoulders and a weight vanished, and yet the stars were made of dense metal and he had them in his eyes, he lowered his head and there it all lay, him too, what time could it be by now, there was no time, everything was departing at once, a slight dizziness, his temples shrinking, the lizards trembled and he could still hear the snoring of the beast, it was a matter of waiting, it pulsed, it had its ways, the beast. There had never been a city down below, feet?, what feet?, he only knew that from the plastic shreds emerged two cats playacting scratches and affection, jumbling their colors, they slipped into two bags and darted out of two others, or was there maybe one cat hidden in every single bag?, he sensed a brush like petals on a muddy path. He abruptly felt even colder and tried to focus on a solitary shard of clouds, a sprig of trimmed plastic gases. The tide was rising.

LXV

The water laps silently against the shore, a falling stone that lingers in suspended, undulating sound. The creaking of the crickets stuns the air, the fireflies knit their little glows together. The myrtles tremble slightly and give off the fragrance of dampened lumber. The cold loses its way inside the woods. The earth thickens until it opens out onto the rocky shore, the water knocking there with silver glints. Against the curtain of the sky, coins spinning on their axis. The ochre of the trunks conceals itself behind the shadows. The thickets twist and curl around oblivion, as a figure in a nightgown, spectral, haunting, quickly cuts through the myrtles like the only happenstance of time stopped still.

LXVI

Demetrio staggered a bit, numb in the ankles, and it seemed to him that the glints of the glass had been a ruse: stars!, they were stars floating like spurs on the lake, it was the punctured surface of the water and suddenly beside the shore there she was, her nightgown shredded and her skin frayed as an old plastic bag, her face dark but still beautiful, meowing, but god, what time was it. At last the papyrus body sank little by little among the bags with a sound like mud and machines, and he heard someone calling his name, once again a familiar muffled murmur, the distant cough of a man who wanted to protect him, and then nothing but the cold, the lake, the breeze made of tiny breezes. Feeling his temples pulse harder, Demetrio picked up his backpack and went with his eyes closed, until, in the middle of the night's expanse, there came the celestial whisper of a dive.

(Granada, November 1996-April 1999
Revised, October 2014-March 2015)

ANDRÉS NEUMAN (1977) was born in Buenos Aires, where he spent his childhood. The son of Argentine émigré musicians, he grew up and lives in Granada, Spain. He has taught Latin American literature at the University of Granada, and was selected as one of *Granta*'s "Best of Young Spanish-Language Novelists." His novel *Traveler of the Century* won the Alfaguara Prize and the National Critics Prize. It was selected among the books of the year by *The Guardian*, *The Independent*, and the *Financial Times*, was shortlisted for the International Dublin Literary Award, and received a Special Commendation from the jury of the Independent Foreign Fiction Prize. His novel *Talking to Ourselves* was longlisted for the 2015 Best Translated Book Award, and shortlisted for the 2015 Oxford-Weidenfeld Translation Prize. His collection of short stories *The Things We Don't Do* won the 2016 Firecracker Award for fiction, given by the Community of Literary Magazines and Presses with the American Booksellers Association. His most recent novels translated into English are *Fracture* and *Bariloche*. An award-winning poet, his selected poems *Love Training* will be coming out soon. His books have been translated into more than twenty languages.

ROBIN MYERS is a poet and Spanish-to-English translator. Her translations include *Salt Crystals* by Cristina Bendek (Charco Press), *Copy* by Dolores Dorantes (Wave Books), *The Dream of Every Cell* by Maricela Guerrero (Cardboard House Press), *The Book of Explanations* by Tedi López Mills (Deep Vellum Publishing), *Cars on Fire* by Mónica Ramón Ríos (Open Letter Books), and *The Restless Dead* by Cristina Rivera Garza (Vanderbilt University Press), among other works of poetry and prose. She was double-longlisted for the 2022 National Translation Award in poetry. She lives in Mexico City.